"Agent Kyle West! FBI!"

The masked man had Ophelia around the throat, even as she thrashed against him. He dragged her toward an open doorway, limping heavily.

Rocky barked wildly, held back only by the fact Kyle hadn't given him the order to leap.

"Let her go!" Kyle raised his weapon. But he couldn't get a clean shot. *Help me, Lord. I can't risk hurting Ophelia.*

"Turn around and leave!" The masked man yanked Ophelia again, and she grabbed his arm and bit down. Her attacker shouted in pain and shoved her hard toward Kyle.

The assailant threw himself through the doorway, into what Kyle now saw was a basement. He was trapped. Rocky snarled.

"Stay here!" Kyle told Ophelia. "We're going after him!"

* * *

Mountain Country K-9 Unit

Baby Protection Mission by Laura Scott, April 2024
Her Duty Bound Defender by Sharee Stover, May 2024
Chasing Justice by Valerie Hansen, June 2024
Crime Scene Secrets by Maggie K. Black, July 2024
Montana Abduction Rescue by Jodie Bailey, August 2024
Trail of Threats by Jessica R. Patch, September 2024
Tracing a Killer by Sharon Dunn, October 2024
Search and Detect by Terri Reed, November 2024
Christmas K-9 Guardians by Lenora Worth and Katy Lee, December 2024

Maggie K. Black is an award-winning journalist and romantic suspense author with an insatiable love of traveling the world. She has lived in the American South, Europe and the Middle East. She now makes her home in Canada with her history-teacher husband, their two beautiful girls and a small but mighty dog. Maggie enjoys connecting with her readers at maggiekblack.com.

Books by Maggie K. Black

Love Inspired Suspense

Undercover Protection
Surviving the Wilderness
Her Forgotten Life
Cold Case Chase
Undercover Baby Rescue

Mountain Country K-9 Unit

Crime Scene Secrets

Unsolved Case Files

Cold Case Tracker

Visit the Author Profile page at LoveInspired.com for more titles.

Crime Scene Secrets

MAGGIE K. BLACK

Special thanks and acknowledgment are given to Maggie K. Black for her contribution to the Mountain Country K-9 Unit miniseries.

PLEASE RECYCLE
THIS PRODUCT IS RECYCLABLE

Recycling programs for this product may not exist in your area.

ISBN-13: 978-1-335-59816-5

Crime Scene Secrets

Love Inspired
22 Adelaide St. West, 41st Floor
Toronto, Ontario M5H 4E3, Canada
www.LoveInspired.com

Printed in Lithuania

Let the words of my mouth, and the meditation
of my heart, be acceptable in thy sight, O Lord,
my strength, and my redeemer.

—*Psalm* 19:14

With thanks to our new fearless series editor, Katie,
for taking all of us on and piloting us through
her first LIS K-9 series

ONE

The sweet scent of yucca flowers filled the warm June air as Ophelia Clarke pulled her car up the narrow Sangre de Cristo Mountains road on the outskirts of Santa Fe, New Mexico. An early sunset spread across the endless sky above her, in a breathtaking array of orange, pink and purple brushstrokes. To her left, a playful goat-shaped sign beckoned her to visit the Cherish Ranch Petting Zoo. Tempting. Instead, she turned right through a large archway that welcomed her to the ranch's wedding venue and the marriage of her second cousin Jared Clarke to his new bride, Gabrielle Martinez.

Rustically elegant adobe buildings seemed to cascade across the mountains ahead of her, their soft, clay-colored walls punctuated by dark wooden beams called vigas. A handful of people mingled, chatted and nibbled on appetizers in a huge courtyard underneath strings of patio lights. A large barn lay beyond it. She parked her small car at the main building, in between two far more lavish vehicles, each of which Ophelia guessed cost more than she made in a year in her job as a crime scene investigator for the Santa Fe PD's Crime Scene Unit. Then she took a deep breath. As much as she loved her cousin Jared, their personalities had never really meshed. She'd always felt far more comfortable stepping under yellow police tape in a full-body white protective jumpsuit than she did standing around hobnobbing with his wealthy friends in a sundress and sandals. Not to mention her beloved great-aunt Evelyn, who was like the grandmother she'd never had, also had an incredible and accidental knack for making her feel inadequate.

Lord, please protect my heart and my mind from getting all hung up on what other people think of me. Even the opinions of well-meaning people I love.

She tossed her long blond hair out around her shoulders, stepped out into the hot, dry air—and heard a voice screaming her name.

"Ophelia!" The woman's panicked voice seemed to be coming from all directions at once. "I'm so glad you're here! There's been a terrible crisis and I need your help!"

Ophelia yanked her phone from her pocket and was about to dial 911 when she saw Gabrielle running down a narrow flight of steps toward her.

"What happened?" Ophelia hastened to her. "Everything okay?"

"No!" Gabrielle shook her head and bell-shaped, yellow yucca flowers tumbled from her intricately braided black hair. "Chloe didn't show up!"

"Who's Chloe?" Ophelia asked. "Is she okay?"

"She's my roommate from Albuquerque!" Gabrielle's well-manicured hand grabbed her by the arm and started dragging her up the steps toward one of the buildings. Words poured from the bride-to-be's lips so quickly Ophelia could barely catch them, let alone make sense of what she was safying. "The rehearsal starts in thirty minutes, but when Nolan went back to the hotel to pick her up Chloe still hadn't checked in yet—"

"Who's Nolan? I don't understand."

"And then I got a text from Chloe saying she wasn't coming to the wedding at all!"

"So she's not here?" Then where was Gabrielle dragging her so quickly? What was she so panicked about? "Where is she? What happened to her?"

"I have no idea!" Gabrielle said. She stopped before a door that seemed to be made of four horizontal planks of wood with huge metal hinges. The sign on it read Wedding Party Only. Gabrielle pushed it open. "Thankfully Jared's grandmother said you'd be happy to rescue me."

"From what?" But the words had barely left Ophelia's lips when she stepped through the doorway and saw the ruffled monstrosity of lavender chiffon that hung alone on a clothes rack in the middle of the room.

Oh, no…

"I told Gabrielle that you'd be happy to help her out of her little crisis." Evelyn's voice rose from the corner of the room. "Aren't you, my dear?"

Ophelia had been so distracted by the purple dress she hadn't even realized her great-aunt was sitting in the corner of the suite. The seventy-four-year-old stood and crossed the floor in a haze of beautifully coiffed gray curls, flowing golden fabric and rose perfume. Now a widow, Evelyn had been a beauty pageant contestant when she was younger, and always dressed impeccably.

"Hello, Auntie, I didn't see you there." Ophelia hugged her gently, her own heart still racing from the fear there'd been an actual emergency. But as they pulled apart she saw a flicker of what seemed to be genuine worry cross her great-aunt's face, and Ophelia felt another twinge of concern.

Hang on, was her great-aunt actually worried about this? Or was there something else going on?

"You sure everything's okay?" Ophelia asked Gabrielle. "When you said there was a crisis, I thought something was actually wrong."

"Of course, something's really wrong." Gabrielle's brown eyes widened and Ophelia couldn't help but notice she was only wearing one contact. "I'm getting married on a cliff-side at sunset tomorrow and one of my bridesmaids didn't show. I can't just have three bridesmaids standing on one side and four groomsmen on the other. It will completely throw off the symmetry."

Symmetry? Ophelia bit the insides of her cheeks and managed to stop herself from snorting.

"I got all the bridesmaids matching heart-shaped lockets to wear," Gabrielle went on. "Sadly, I've already given Chloe hers, but it's too late to do anything about that now. I guess this means none of the other bridesmaids will get to wear theirs, either, so your outfits match." She sighed. "Of course, you're welcome to stay in Chloe's hotel room. It's a five-star hotel and I'd love to have the whole wedding party staying together. Now, there isn't any way you can rustle up a date for yourself, can you? Jared told me you're hopelessly single, but it'll also throw off the seating plan if you don't have a date."

Hopelessly single? She was a thirty-one-year-old career woman, not some teenager in a 1950s movie who'd just been dumped on prom night. Ophelia felt her jaw clench. She hadn't wanted to be a bridesmaid in the first place and now this whole thing was snowballing. It was just one weekend, she reminded herself. And this was family. She'd just grin and bear it. By tomorrow night it would all be over. "No, I won't be bringing a date," Ophelia said.

Gabrielle's lips turned down in a pretty pout.

"I'm sorry, but did you know you're missing a contact?" Ophelia added. "Do you need help finding it?"

"Wow, you're right!" Gabrielle blinked twice and then laughed. "What an odd thing to even notice about someone! I guess I've been so distracted with wedding plans I didn't realize."

"Sorry," Ophelia said automatically, then wasn't exactly sure why she was apologizing for trying to be helpful. "It's a hazard of my job. I'm used to noticing the little things. You never know when one victim's missing contact is the key to catching a serial killer."

She meant it as a joke, but Gabrielle didn't laugh. Out of the corner of her eye, Ophelia could see her great-aunt frantically signaling her to drop the topic. She definitely seemed a bit more on edge than usual.

"But Jared said you were some kind of science nerd who worked with animals?" Gabrielle asked.

"Well, I'm working on a PhD in using DNA markers to help track the endangered Rocky Mountain wolf population," Ophelia said, "and also working full-time for Santa Fe PD's Crime Scene Unit."

In fact, she'd received a wonderful financial grant that covered most of her studies, so most of her salary could go to covering her day-to-day living expenses. She'd always felt passionate about conservation but had also realized pretty quickly during her undergraduate science degree that her greatest strengths lay in the lab. Now all she had to do was successfully juggle her work with her research, and she'd be able to fulfill both her dreams of being a CSI and doing life-changing research. It just meant hitting some pretty tight PhD deadlines that often had her researching and writing late into the night. She barely had time to eat and sleep, let alone think about finding a date for her second cousin's wedding.

"Ophelia has always loved animals," Evelyn said, "and I'm sure she won't mind stepping in as an emergency bridesmaid." She turned to her great-niece. "Do you, Ophelia?" Evelyn asked, firmly.

"No, of course not, Auntie." Although Jared had promised he wouldn't try to rope her into the wedding party. Ophelia and Jared were both only children and, despite their differences, were the closest thing each had to a sibling. With the same blond hair and blue eyes, they even looked like brother and sister. Ophelia's parents had traveled a lot for work and her own grandmother had died before she was born. Evelyn had stepped in, inviting her to spend every holiday and vacation with her and Jared. Ophelia could do this much for them.

"See, I knew this would be sorted out," Evelyn said, turning to smile at Gabrielle. "Ophelia's been a bridesmaid more times than I can count."

"Four, actually," Ophelia said softly. "This will be number five."

She was practically an expert at smiling uncomfortably in a dress she'd have never chosen for herself, while standing next to a beamingly happy couple.

"Five times," Evelyn said brightly. "You know what they say—"

Please, don't say it.

"Always a bridesmaid, never a bride!" Evelyn said. "You know, I worry sometimes that nobody's going to marry this one. Which would be a shame, because Ophelia is so wonderful and I love her like my own grandchild. I thank God every day for bringing her and Jared into my life."

That was her great-aunt in a nutshell—accidental insults and a genuine compliment in the same breath.

Evelyn waved her hand toward Gabrielle. "Now go visit with your guests. Ophelia and I will see how the dress fits."

"Thank you so much for this. I owe you one." Gabrielle disappeared out the door and closed it behind her.

Evelyn sighed. "I wish you wouldn't do that."

"Do what?" Ophelia pulled the dress off the hanger and disappeared with it into the adjoining room. The sooner she got trying the dress on over with, the sooner she could go join the party.

"Talk about things like murders and crime scenes," Evelyn said. "It's impolite. Besides, you never know who you're going to meet at an event like this, and no man wants to marry a woman who pokes around in blood and guts for a living."

"Which is why I expect I'll never get married," Ophelia called, lightly. A few minutes later she emerged again in layers of flowing purple fabric and did a little spin. "Thankfully, the dress isn't terrible."

Her great-aunt looked her up and down, critically.

"No, it's not," she conceded and dropped into a chair. "Which is a relief, considering."

"Considering what?" What exactly was Evelyn concerned about? Ophelia knelt down beside her. "Auntie, what's wrong? You can tell me."

"Absolutely nothing you need to worry about," she said firmly. "Gabrielle's parents are just running late because their flight from Europe was delayed due to a storm. So

Jared just needed some help sorting some money things with the venue. You know they're buying Jared and Gabrielle a piece of land near the Pecos Wilderness as a wedding present?"

"Yes," Ophelia said, "he took me up there a few weeks ago to show me, before he put the offer in. Got my help to tie balloons to the trees for when he took her up to surprise her with it. Said they were going to build a house there 'where the mountains meet the sky.' It was all terribly theatrical." The land had been beautiful but completely undeveloped, except for a small shack the previous owners had left behind, but the views had been extraordinary. "Is there some problem with the land?"

"Oh, I'm sure it's nothing." Evelyn waved her hands airily as if batting away invisible cobwebs. "There was just a minor hiccup with the initial down payment, due to restrictions on foreign buyers, so he had to step in and cover it. They'll pay him back. Plus, this whole wedding has just been so lavish."

Evelyn pressed her lips together as if she'd been about to say more and caught herself.

"Are Jared and Gabrielle struggling for money?" Ophelia asked. "I thought he had an excellent job."

"He does and everything's fine," Evelyn said, with a tone that Ophelia knew meant that even if it wasn't, she was changing the topic. "You should really consider staying with us in the hotel. The rooms they've booked are just gorgeous. Now, I have a plan to get you a date for this wedding. One of my friends told me about this wonderful telephone thing she used to help her grandson find a wife."

"That's kind, but I'm not looking to date anyone right now. Between my full-time job and a PhD, I don't really have time."

But Evelyn had already gone to get her large cell phone from her purse. She opened it to a bubble gum pink dating app. Ophelia gaped as her grandmother started to swipe through the smiling faces.

"It's called Loving Meddlers," Evelyn said. Her blue eyes twinkled. "Isn't that perfect? You can put your grown children and grandchildren on it, and it shows you lovely young people nearby who you can introduce them to, through whoever put them on the thing. Like, see, this man's mother just logged in that they're visiting a petting zoo less than a quarter of a mile away. He's a cop and has a little boy."

Ophelia glanced down at the screen and felt a rush of heat rising to her cheeks, to see the dark hair and intense brown eyes of FBI Agent Kyle West of the Mountain Country K-9 Task Force looking back up at her. Ophelia bit her lower lip as if the incredibly handsome detective could see her through the screen.

"I actually know that one," she admitted, "or at least I know of him. We've worked several of the same crime scenes. He's an FBI agent who specializes in serial killers."

"Oh." Evelyn grimaced. "Maybe not him, then."

A loud bang sounded from somewhere on the other side of the door. Instinctively, Ophelia froze. A second bang sounded. A distant voice screamed.

"Is somebody setting off fireworks?" Evelyn asked.

"No." Ophelia could feel a danger warning tingling at the back of her skull. "Those were gunshots." The property didn't have a range and handguns were prohibited for hunting in Santa Fe. She snatched up her bag, opened the door a crack and listened. Voices were shouting in what sounded like panic and confusion. "Stay here and don't open the door to anyone but me or Jared."

"Don't be ridiculous, sweetie," her great-aunt called. "If there's something wrong it'll be handled by law enforcement."

"I'm a part of law enforcement."

One without a gun, but still she wasn't about to just hunker down and hide when someone might be in danger.

She locked the door handle behind her and slipped back out into the heat. The courtyard was empty, leaving nothing but fallen chairs and plates of food. The gunshot and scream seemed to have been coming from the direction of the barn where the wedding reception would be. She made her way toward it, gleaning what bits of information she could from the shaken guests she passed.

Then she saw Jared running toward her in an expensive tan suit, his eyes wide with panic. He grabbed her arm. "Ophelia!"

"Are you okay?" she asked.

"Have you seen Gabrielle?"

"No," she said. "But your grandmother is safe and inside one of the suites."

His blue eyes scanned past her. He still hadn't answered her question and she wondered if he'd even heard her.

"What happened?" she asked.

"I don't know." His skin was paler than she'd ever seen it before and so clammy she wondered if he was about to be sick. "I heard this popping sound. People dropped their food and ran into the building. Somebody said someone was shot."

"Who?"

"I don't know," he said. "But I heard someone scream."

"I did, too," she said. "Has anyone called 911?"

"I…I don't know…" His head shook. She wondered if he was in shock. "I have to find Gabrielle."

"When you find her, get inside!"

In the meantime, she was going to call 911. She dialed the number and ran for the barn, down stone paths hemmed in by tall, flowering bushes. A dispatcher answered immediately.

"This is CSI Ophelia Clarke of the Santa Fe PD," Ophelia told her. "I'm at Cherish Ranch's wedding venue in the Sangre de Cristo Mountains. I heard gunfire and there's a report of someone being shot. I'm trying to find that person and see if I can help them."

And if not, she was going to secure the scene and keep people from trampling on whatever evidence there was. Her sandals slipped on the terra-cotta tile, threatening to trip her up. She kicked them off and ran for the barn barefoot.

"We've got law enforcement heading your way," the dispatcher told her. "But they're twenty-two minutes out."

Which might be too late if the victim was bleeding out. And an eternity if the shooter was still on-site.

"Call FBI Agent Kyle West of the Mountain Country K-9 Task Force," Ophelia said. "He's apparently less than a quarter mile away."

"We'll try to reach him."

She silently thanked God for her great-aunt's ridiculous app for alerting her to that. Ophelia reached the barn. A handful of guests were standing around the front, taking pictures on their phones, while a couple of men in suits, who she guessed were ranch security, tried to stop them from getting too close.

She wedged her phone into the crook of her neck, yanked her identification badge from her bag and flashed it at them.

"CSI Clarke, Santa Fe PD," she said. "I'm on the phone with dispatch now."

They waved her through. The huge sliding door was open a couple of feet. She came to a stop.

"Hello?" she called. No answer.

She took a deep breath to steal her nerves and stepped inside. The barn was deep and cool. Chandeliers constructed from hundreds of vintage lightbulbs hung down from the ceiling above. Tables were stacked along one side, covered with mason jar oil lamps. Chairs decked in flowing fabric sat in clumps waiting to be set up for the reception, along with pedestals of flowers and buckets of soapy water and cleaning supplies. Silently, she tiptoed through them.

Then she saw him.

The man lay on the floor behind an empty cake stand. He was tall, blond, casually dressed in a T-shirt and jeans, and dead from a gunshot wound to the chest.

"Down!" Brody said. The toddler wriggled in Kyle's arms and waved his hands toward the scampering baby goats as Kyle stepped through the gate to the Cherish Ranch Petting Zoo's goat pen and closed the gate behind them. "Want pat!"

Kyle chuckled.

"Me, too, buddy." He knelt down, set the little boy on the ground and held him steady with one arm strong around his waist, knowing that otherwise he'd run off and try to climb on the very same wooden climbing frame the tiny hooves now balanced on. "But I'm not sure any of them are going to stay still long enough for that."

It had been a long afternoon at the petting zoo. They'd finished their picnic dinner and the sun had begun to set. But still, Brody's energy level hadn't even begun to flag.

Keeping up with his nephew had been an adjustment since he'd been unexpectedly thrust into single fatherhood after his brother and sister-in-law had passed. With green eyes and a mop of curly dark hair, Brody was the spitting image of his father, Kevin. Kyle's heart ached with the thought of how Brody's parents would miss seeing the little boy grow up. Thankfully, he had the help of his widowed mother, Alice West, who had moved in to help raise Brody. Together, the three remaining Wests had formed a small, fractured family.

Kyle's phone buzzed in his pocket. Jostling around the squirming toddler, Kyle reached in, fished it out and glanced at the screen. It was his Mountain Country K-9 Team Leader, Chase Rawlston. Kyle sent it through to voice mail and made a mental note to check it later. Chase had promised Kyle a week off to spend with his family, and Kyle had been determined not to let anything get in the way of spending time with Brody.

It had barely been two weeks since Kyle had gotten back from assisting Selena Smith, a sheriff's deputy in Sagebrush, Idaho, and a member of the Mountain Country K-9 Task Force, in protecting a targeted convict. And while, thankfully, the case had been closed and the convict found to be innocent, the entire MCK9 Task Force was still working flat out to catch a pernicious serial killer—dubbed the Rocky Mountain Killer—who'd murdered six people so far across Wyoming, Montana and Colorado. The RMK had also managed to evade them.

"I can pat!" Brody declared confidently. He stretched his tiny fingers out toward a small kid with black-and-white fur and tiny curling gray horns. "Come here, pat!"

"He definitely doesn't lack confidence, does he, Kyle?" Alice West chuckled.

Kyle turned and looked through the fence, to where Brody's grandmother stood, holding the dogs' leashes. With her long gray hair in twin braids and clad in blue jeans and cowboy boots, his sixty-two-year-old mother had a deep faith and perpetual joy that belied the tragedy of having been married to an abusive man and then losing her eldest son. To Alice's right sat Kyle's K-9 partner, Rocky, a magnificent black-and-tan hunting hound who specialized in cadaver detection, especially in the rough and hilly terrain of the Rocky Mountains. Rocky watched the goats, with his head cocked and his long, velvety ears attuned to any sign of trouble. Rocky's half sister, Taffy—a three-month-old puppy who was the spitting image of her big brother—was tangled up in the leash as she tried to run in multiple directions at once. Kyle had adopted her as a family dog when the puppy's sweet but goofy temperament had been deemed to be unsuitable for the rigors of K-9 training. Truth was that most days he felt more like Taffy than Rocky.

It had been over a year since Brody's parents—Kyle's brother Kevin and wife, Caitlyn—had died when their small helicopter had suddenly gotten caught in a treacherous thunderstorm in the Rocky Mountains. To Kyle's surprise, Brody's parents had specifically mentioned in their will that their hope was Kyle would adopt Brody and become his father if anything ever happened to them.

"He reminds me of Kevin," Alice added. His mother's smile faded as the words froze on her lips. An old familiar ache turned in Kyle's chest.

"Me, too," Kyle said wistfully. His fraternal twin might've

only been six minutes older, but he'd been Kyle's hero and filled with a strength and confidence Kyle could only hope to find.

Lord, I feel like I'm never going to be able to fill the hole left in this little boy's life. Please guide me in Your path.

His phone buzzed again. Kyle frowned. Chase was calling back.

"Do you need to get that?" his mother asked.

"Yeah, I probably should." He scooped Brody up into his arms and stood, despite the boy's wails of protest, and carried him back out of the goat pen. "He knows it's my week off, so hopefully nothing's wrong."

Deftly Alice handed him Rocky's leash with one hand, while taking her still-protesting grandson into her arms. "We're going to go get ice cream. Come find us when you're done or give me a shout if you've got to run."

"Will do. Thanks, Mom."

She waved a hand for him to go, and he silently thanked God for her.

Kyle glanced down at his partner. Rocky's serious dark eyes looked up at him, silently asking him what was going on. Yeah, he wondered that, too.

He started toward the privacy of the parking lot, with his partner at his side, and answered the phone.

"Kyle here," he said. "Hey, Chase, what's up?"

"Hey," Chase said. His boss sounded a bit tired, but with every ounce of the same determined grit Kyle had come to appreciate from the task force leader. A supervisory special agent with the FBI, Chase had lost his wife and child in a revenge bombing in DC five years ago. A lesser man might've packed up his badge and given up his faith along with it. Chase had moved back to Elk Valley to work in the

Wyoming bureau, before heading up the task force Kyle was so proud to be a part of. "Sorry to bother you on your week off, but there's been a report from Santa Fe PD about an incident at the Cherish Ranch wedding venue in Sangre de Cristo Mountains. Guests reported hearing gunshots. Victim was found in the barn, male in his twenties, with a single gunshot to the chest."

That was the Rocky Mountain Killer's MO.

"But the crime scene investigator, who was first on-site, told dispatch that you were in the area and requested you by name," Chase added.

"I'm at the petting zoo next door." But he had no idea how anyone would know that. He and Rocky jogged toward his truck. The cell signal crackled and he hoped it wouldn't cut out. Phone reception wasn't the best here in the mountains and made worse by the fact that he was on the move. "I'm on my way and two minutes out. Who requested me?"

"A CSI Clarke."

An unexpected wave of relief washed over him. "Oh, she's excellent."

In the year or so since he'd come into contact with Ophelia Clarke, Kyle had quickly pegged her as the very best investigator he'd ever worked with. Her work was both thorough and meticulous. Not that Kyle thought they'd ever exchanged two words. Or, come to think of it, even knew what Ophelia looked like under her full-body protective gear, booties and mask. But between the old-fashioned name and her excellent work, he'd always envisioned her as being around the same age as his mom, with curly gray hair, a sharp gaze and well-disciplined grandchildren.

Kyle knew nothing would be missed whenever he saw Ophelia Clarke's name on a case.

"Got it." Kyle opened the back door of his SUV for Rocky. The dog leaped into the back seat and lay down. Kyle hopped in the front and plugged his phone into the vehicle's hands-free system.

"Do we know if it's connected to the RMK?" he asked.

"That's what I'm hoping you'll be able to find out," Chase said.

It had been a decade since three young men had been found shot dead in Elk Valley, Wyoming, on Valentine's Day night. The three friends had all been members of the Young Rancher's Club, known to local police as trouble-makers and lured to a barn by a flirtatious text from a burner phone. They'd been shot—each with a gunshot wound to the chest. The murder weapon had never been found, but ballistics had matched the 9mm slugs. The case had gone cold for ten years until, four months ago, two more men were found shot the same way, one in Colorado and another in Montana. Then recently a sixth victim was found in Idaho. Every weapon left its own unique pattern of ridges and marks on each bullet it fired. CSI had determined the three bullets found at the new crime scenes, and those from the original murders, had not only been fired from the same type of gun, but the exact same gun.

Could this new shooting be connected?

"Santa Fe PD and paramedics are fourteen minutes out," Chase added. "You and CSI Clarke are the first on the scene."

"Understood."

Thank You, Lord, that CSI Clarke was there. Please help us get the evidence we need to stop the RMK and crack his case.

"Let's meet up via video call tomorrow morning at eight,"

Chase went on. "I'm going to ask Isla to join us, too, and maybe others. If this does turn out to be related to the RMK, I want to make sure you have the backup you need."

"Sounds good." The MCK9 Task Force's technical analyst, Isla Jimenez, was second to none and someone Kyle was thankful to call a friend.

"I'll also coordinate with the Santa Fe PD," Chase went on, "as I'm sure it'll end up being a joint investigation if there is a RMK connection. But at the moment it's too soon to know anything really."

"Understood. Talk soon."

They ended the call. Kyle sent his mom a quick text letting her know that he had to work a scene nearby and would be in touch later. Then he peeled out of the crowded petting zoo parking lot as quickly as he safely could and followed a small sign directing him to the wedding venue. In a matter of moments, he pulled through an arch welcoming him to the wedding of Jared Clarke and Gabrielle Martinez. The top of the rustic barn appeared ahead through pine trees. He drove through the parking lot and down a small access road. He stopped the vehicle as close as he could to the barn, got his badge and gun from his glove compartment, then hopped out and ran down the winding path, with Rocky by his side.

There wasn't another emergency vehicle in sight. But a couple of men in crisp black suits and sunglasses, who he guessed were ranch security, were standing by the entrance, holding back a small gaggle of well-dressed gawkers in pastel dresses and paisley ties, who seemed to be trying to film whatever they could with their phones.

He held up his badge and identified himself to the security officer closest to the door.

"FBI Agent Kyle West, Mountain Country K-9 Task Force," he said. "Has anyone been inside?"

"No, sir." The guard shook his head. "Just the chick."

Chick?

He couldn't imagine anyone referring to Ophelia Clarke like that. Had one of the party guests breached the perimeter? Whoever he was talking about, she shouldn't be in there.

"We need a twenty-five-foot perimeter around this barn," Kyle said. "Get everyone out of here and keep them back. They'll all need to be questioned. The priority is figuring out where everyone was at the time the gunshots were fired and not giving anyone the opportunity to coordinate their stories." Not to mention, the last thing he needed were people trampling all over the evidence or crime scene pictures ending up on social media. "Make sure the entrance is clear for emergency services when they get here."

The guards nodded and started yelling for people to get back. Kyle signaled Rocky to stay close to his side and started for the door. The double barn door seemed designed to open all the way on both sides, but for now it was only open a couple of feet. For someone to slip in and out without being seen? A soft growl rumbled in the back of Rocky's throat, letting him know that death lay on the other side. Kyle pulled his weapon.

"Agent Kyle West, Mountain Country K-9 Task Force," he called. "Drop your weapons and get down on the ground with your hands up."

"It's clear," a female voice called. "He's already dead."

"I'm sorry, ma'am," he said. "You really can't be in here. I'm going to have to ask you to leave."

He stepped through the door and froze. The most beautiful woman he'd ever seen knelt on the floor in a flowing purple dress beside the bloodied body of a man in jeans and a T-shirt. She seemed to be checking the corpse's pockets.

"No wallet, no phone and no identification," she said, as if he hadn't just politely told her to leave. "We seem to have a John Doe."

She tossed her long blond hair around her shoulders and stood. Dazzling blue eyes fixed on his face. He felt his mouth open and close again, like a goldfish.

"Single gunshot wound to the torso," she went on. "Pretty much dead center and still imbedded in his chest. I checked his vitals and attempted CPR. But I'm afraid he's gone."

She ran her hands down her skirt, leaving bloody streaks on the delicate fabric. Only then did he notice she was wearing plastic gloves. She looked down at them as if debating extending a hand to shake his, before deciding against it. "I'm glad you got my message."

He holstered his weapon. "I'm sorry, who are you?"

"Ophelia Clarke." Something hardened in the blue of her eyes. Her chin rose. "Crime Scene Investigator for the Santa Fe PD's Crime Scene Unit. It's good to see you again, Agent West."

He just stood there and blinked, while his brain struggled to compute the fact that the most impressive crime scene tech he'd ever worked with also just happened to be the most beautiful woman he'd ever seen. *Come on, man*, he chided himself. He'd worked with a lot of strong and talented female officers, detectives, agents and CSIs for his entire career. So, what was it about this particular one that had suddenly robbed his tongue of its ability to form words?

"The groom is my second cousin," Ophelia added. She pulled her gloves off. "I came for the rehearsal party and they were trying to rope me in as a bridesmaid, when I heard the gunshots. Thankfully I always keep a few gloves and evidence bags in my purse." Ophelia glanced at his partner and a warm smile crossed her face. "Hello, Rocky."

She ran her hand down his side. His partner's tail thumped against the floor. Seemed Rocky had no problem recognizing her.

"I'm so sorry," he said. "I didn't recognize you without the protective gear. I assumed you were a guest who'd just wandered in and started playing detective."

He'd meant it as a joke, but she didn't smile.

"I'm glad you're here, too," he plowed on, hoping to find the right thing to say to put the investigation back on track. "You're a really good CSI."

"Uh, thank you?" Now it was her turn to blink.

Had he said something else wrong? Or was she just not used to being complimented? Either way, it seemed he'd managed to put his foot in it again.

Then she glanced past him and her face paled.

"There's a man in a mask in the trees," she said. "He's got a gun pointed right at the barn."

Before he could turn, a gunshot sounded and the barn door behind him exploded into splinters.

TWO

"Take cover!" Kyle shouted. "Rocky, stay low!"

But Ophelia froze, her body suddenly too paralyzed by fear to move. She felt Kyle throw his strong and protective arms around her. He cradled her to his chest as they fell together to the ground. In one strong kick, Kyle brought a flower pedestal crashing down in front of them, creating a limited barrier between them and the man outside, just as the gunman let off a second shot. This one ricocheted across the floor.

For a second she lay there on the ground, with one of Kyle's arms around her shoulder and her heart beating painfully in her chest. Kyle pulled away, unholstered his weapon and rolled up to a crouching position.

Then it hit her. "Kyle, there are people out there!"

"Not anymore," he said. "I asked security to create a wide perimeter. Everybody should be out of harm's way, except us."

Thank You, God.

She glanced around. Rocky was crawling toward the cover of a stack of tables to their right. The gunman was a tall and indistinct form, with a black baseball cap on over his ski mask. Some kind of dark mesh covered the eyeholes, so she couldn't even clock the color of his eyes. He raised his handgun and fired. A third and fourth shot sounded in quick succession. A chandelier crashed down from somewhere above, sending broken glass cascading across the floor.

What did the assailant think he was doing? He wasn't firing at them. She wasn't sure he even knew they were there. It was more like he was treating the barn as his personal shooting gallery.

"We've got to move," Kyle said. "Can you crawl?"

"I think so." She gritted her teeth and grabbed her bag. "If not, just drag me until my limbs decide to cooperate."

He snorted. "Will do. We're heading for the tables by the wall. Just follow Rocky."

She rolled over onto her hands and knees and started for the spot where Rocky was now sheltered under the tables, thankful that her body seemed to have finally agreed to become unstuck. Kyle positioned himself between her and the gunman and matched her pace. When they reached the tables, once again she felt Kyle's protective hand brush her shoulder. His dark eyes scanned her as silently he checked her face.

"I'm okay," she said. "Thank you."

"Thank You, God," he murmured.

Amen. Thank You that Kyle was here. Thank You for my safety. Please keep anyone else from being harmed.

Then Kyle moved away from her, pulled out his phone and started talking. She assumed he was contacting emergency services. Rocky crawled over beside her and gave her fingers a reassuring lick. She ran her hand over his head. The hound was almost entirely black except for his tan snout and paws. She always had a soft spot for the beautiful canine with his long, silky ears and serious eyes.

"Backup is six minutes out," Kyle called.

In the meantime, it was almost as if the gunman was intentionally trashing the scene. A bucket full of soapy water went flying, sending suds cascading across the floor.

"He's destroying evidence!" Ophelia shouted.

Kyle pulled the phone from his ear. "You mean on purpose?"

"Maybe. I don't know."

But she hadn't thought to start snapping pictures when she'd arrived, or even take notes. She'd been too focused on seeing if she could save the victim's life. And now the only record of what she'd observed when she first arrived on the scene existed solely in her mind.

She could now hear the faint sound of sirens in the distance. Kyle's attention had turned back to the phone again. Impulsively, she grabbed Kyle's free hand and squeezed it. His eyes snapped back to her face.

"Listen to me," she said urgently. "He's destroying evidence and I didn't take pictures, so I need you to remember everything I'm about to tell you."

"Will do," he replied, without question.

She closed her eyes and prayed.

Lord, help me remember what I need to.

"The barn door was open only a couple of feet when I got here," she said, keeping her eyes closed in concentration. "I don't think the lights were on, but there was enough daylight to see. I didn't notice any obvious signs of a struggle. No broken glass, no overturned furniture, nothing spilled, nothing in disarray."

"Got it," he said. She felt him squeeze her hand. "Go on."

"I didn't see the body until I stepped in a few feet. He was partially blocked by planters. He was dressed casually in jeans and a green T-shirt. One bullet wound, fatal and close range." She opened her eyes. His dark gaze was locked on her face and she realized his hand was still enveloping hers. She pulled away. "My job is to focus on gathering evidence. Your job is to interpret it. But if I had to guess, he knew his killer."

"I'd go a step further and say the victim was probably looking him dead in the eye when he was shot," Kyle added, dryly. "Have you heard of the Rocky Mountain Killer?"

"Vaguely."

"He lured all his victims into barns and shot them at point-blank range. Six so far. Maybe, this guy is number seven."

"Well, I didn't see any evidence that our John Doe wasn't lured here," she said.

"Yeah," Kyle said. "Only question is why didn't the killer choose a more isolated location."

Ophelia scanned the room, silently praying that she'd remember anything important that she hadn't focused on.

A glimmer of something gold caught her eye. The item was slightly smaller than a bullet. Just a few feet away from the next table over and seemed to shine in the refracted light of the glass on the floor surrounding it. The gunman fired ahead. A table full of kerosene mason jar lamps shattered, sending the pungent fuel pouring down inches away from the object.

Ophelia didn't even hesitate. She yanked a fresh pair of gloves from her purse, slid them on and grabbed an empty evidence bag. Then she slowly crawled under the next table over.

"What are you doing?" Kyle asked, sharply.

"I'm rescuing evidence!"

"That's not your job!"

To crawl into the line of fire to rescue a shiny object from a murder scene? Maybe not, but it was close enough.

"Stop!" Kyle called. "Get back here."

For a moment she wondered if he was actually going to grab her ankles and try pulling her back. But it was too late; she was already ducking her head out and slithering on her stomach across the floor. A second later, her fingers wrapped around the object. She ducked back under the table and dropped the item into the bag, just as another gunshot sounded.

In an instant, Kyle was at her side. They crouched side by side below the table.

"What were you thinking?" he asked. "You could've been killed."

"But I wasn't." And hopefully had rescued a clue. She held up the evidence bag. Together they peered at it. His shoulder brushed hers. It was a cuff link. So shiny it looked new and yet also marred with what appeared to be the victim's blood. "Why would a man in a T-shirt and jeans have cuff links with him?" she asked.

"I have no idea."

"There's some kind of inscription on it. But between the blood and the small, stylized letters, I'm having a hard time reading it." She squinted. "Looks like an *R*. The second letter might be an *H*, an *N* or an *M*. I'm not sure. And I can't make out the third."

The sirens roared even closer. Kyle's back stiffened. "Could the letters be *RMK*?"

"Maybe," she said. "Definitely, looks like it. Why? What does that mean?"

"It means this murder very well could be the work of that

serial killer I mentioned," he said, "and the Rocky Mountain Killer might be the man shooting at us now."

A cold chill ran down Kyle's spine as he glanced to the masked figure, praying God would give him the opportunity to get a clean shot. Instead, he watched as the shooter turned tail and took off running through the trees.

But Kyle wasn't about to let him get away. The MCK9 Task Force had been tracking the killer for months.

"I'm going after him," he called. "Stay low and stay safe. Backup will be here any second."

"I'll be fine," Ophelia called. "Just go!"

He slid out from under the table, summoned Rocky to his side and took off sprinting through the barn and out into the mountain air. To his right he could see the flashing lights of police cars and ambulances lighting up the sky. The sound of voices shouting just beyond the hedges told him backup was moments away.

But he didn't let himself break stride. Instead, he and Rocky dove through the pine trees and juniper bushes, after the departing figure. The ground sloped steeply. Loose rocks tumbled beneath their feet, threatening to send them falling. He could barely see the figure through the forest. But he could hear the sound of brush branches snapping beneath his feet. The sun was setting lower in the sky now. Soon it would disappear beneath the horizon altogether, leaving an inky blue darkness behind.

Then suddenly the trees parted and Kyle could see him.

The figure was at least six feet tall, stocky and strong. A sheer cliff lay ahead of him, jutting out into the air.

"Stop!" Kyle shouted. He raised his weapon. "FBI!"

But the man vaulted over the edge and disappeared from view.

Kyle pressed faster. He and Rocky raced to the edge and looked down, just in time to see the masked man scrambling down to the bottom of a steep slope. An expensive-looking silver car stood on the road beneath it. The man dove into it and Kyle fired, catching him in the left calf. Shouting and swearing loudly in pain, the man struggled as he slammed the car door. Kyle set the vehicle in his sights and fired, just as the engine roared to life. The back window shattered.

The car sped off around a bend and out of sight.

Kyle re-holstered his weapon. Then he pulled out his phone to call dispatch and told them to be on the lookout for a man with a gunshot wound to the left calf and a silver car with a broken back window. But he couldn't get a signal. He groaned.

He lifted his gaze to where the golden sun was disappearing, leaving just a sliver of light at the edge of the horizon.

Lord, whether that man is the RMK, an accomplice of his or not connected to the other murders at all, please help me catch him and bring him to justice. And guide everyone else involved in the investigation.

He looked down at Rocky. The dog whimpered sympathetically and bumped his head against Kyle's side. Kyle chuckled and ran his hand along his partner's neck.

"You are a very good dog," he said. "It's not your fault he got away. You weren't trained for that, and you're excellent at what you are trained for." Which was finding the dead, not only giving law enforcement the evidence needed to bring the killers to justice, but also bringing peace and closure to the friends and family left behind. "Now come on, let's get back to the crime scene and see what the witnesses can tell us about the John Doe in the barn."

They turned and jogged through the trees toward the ranch. Truth was, when Kyle had joined the FBI's K-9 Unit, he'd envisioned himself partnered with the kind of imposing beast who'd help him physically chase down killers. He'd never expected to be paired with an animal who was so patient, dedicated and diligent in finding victims instead. But the moment he'd laid eyes on the two-foot-tall, black-and-tan hound, something in his heart had known that he and Rocky were meant to work together to find those whose bodies had been lost. It was a sobering job, one filled with a lot of sadness, but also a lot of hope and the certainty they were making a difference.

And Kyle thanked God for his partner every day.

It was no surprise that his son, Brody, was absolutely besotted with Rocky, too, and would charge across the room to throw his little arms around the dog whenever they came home from work, while Rocky sat patiently and accepted the small boy's enthusiastic squeezes with a gentle lick. Brody had been beside himself with joy when Taffy had joined the family as well, giving him a pint-size canine playmate who stayed home with him when Kyle and Rocky went off to work.

Kyle had felt blindsided by happiness when he'd first cradled Brody in his arms, a few hours after the little boy's birth. He never could've imagined the tragedy that would lead to him adopting Brody just six months later, when the child was too young to even understand what had happened. Kyle could also never understand why Kevin and Caitlyn had specified in their will that they wanted Kyle to adopt their son in the event of their deaths, when they had so many incredible friends, many of whom were already married with kids of their own.

How could they possibly be sure that he was the right man to be Brody's father? He was an expert in catching serial killers, who'd never had a serious girlfriend and whose K-9 partner tracked the dead.

Lord, I love Brody with all my heart and there's never been a doubt in my mind that I want to be his dad. I just worry I'm going to let him down.

After all, his own father had been a brute. He couldn't imagine the courage it had taken Kevin to get married and start a family, considering they'd hardly had a decent role model.

He could see law enforcement's flashing lights ahead and followed them back to the barn. He couldn't have been gone more than fifteen minutes, but already yellow police tape surrounded the scene and the chaos of the barn had been taken over by a small army of CSI agents in white protective gear. He scanned the scene for Ophelia but couldn't spot her.

"Agent West!" a woman's voice called to him from within the cordoned-off area.

"Over here!"

He turned toward the sound. It was Detective Patricia Gonzales, a senior investigator within the Santa Fe Police Department and one of the most dedicated officers Kyle had ever had the privilege of working with. She was in her early sixties, he guessed, not that he'd ever risk asking. Her black hair was streaked with white and tied back in a crisp bun.

"Detective Gonzales!" As he strode toward the police tape, a Santa Fe PD officer lifted it up and let him through. "It's good to see you."

"Likewise." She nodded at him and Rocky in greeting. "I heard you were the first investigator on the scene."

"I was," he said, "after CSI Clarke, who was on-site for a family event, found the body and called it in."

All of which she'd already know. He quickly filled her in on the suspect he'd been pursuing, the fact that he'd managed to clip him in the left leg, the silver car with the shattered back window and that Kyle hadn't yet been able to call it in. Then he waited while she contacted dispatch and told them to be on the lookout for the suspect and vehicle. Then she turned back to Kyle.

"And what's the Country Mountain K-9 Task Force's link to this case?" she asked.

"I was close to the scene, so they called me in. But the shooting seems to match the MO of the Rocky Mountain Killer," he said. "Male victim, in a barn, with a single gunshot to his chest."

"A lot of people get shot in barns," Patricia said. She sounded skeptical.

"True," he said. A lot of people got shot in the chest, too.

"I thought all those killings took place in Wyoming," she added, "and the victims were connected to some Young Rancher's Club."

"The first three murders were in Elk Valley, Wyoming, ten years ago," he said. "The next three were more recent, in Idaho, Montana and Colorado. All were connected by a party the Elk Valley Young Rancher's Club had a decade ago."

"And all those states are on a pretty straight line down the I-25 Highway to Santa Fe," Patricia said. "We've got no ID on the victim yet. Do we know if anyone from this wedding was connected to this Young Rancher's Club?"

"No," Kyle said. But he was looking forward to finding out. "My mother and son are at the petting zoo. Do you know if I have any reason to be concerned for them?"

"No," Patricia said, and he appreciated her bluntness. "Not at all. We have no reason to believe anyone there is in danger or was impacted."

He breathed a sigh of relief. "Yeah, I couldn't even hear the shots from there."

"We do have an officer on-site checking vehicles on the way in and out of the petting zoo," the detective added. "I'd be happy to get someone to pick your family up and escort them home, if you'd like."

"Actually, could you get someone to drop my SUV off to them at the petting zoo?" Kyle asked. It was past Brody's bedtime; Kyle had a hunch that he was going to be here awhile and was sure he could get a ride home.

"Will do."

Kyle sent off a quick text to his mom, who wrote back right away, telling him not to worry and that she'd put Brody to bed, but that Kyle would have to sort breakfast as she had to run some early morning errands. He thanked his mom and then he silently thanked God for her.

As Chase had suggested would happen, Patricia said that for now they'd proceed with the case as a joint investigation between the local Santa Fe Police Department and the Mountain Country K-9 Task Force. Which was good by Kyle. He was the only MCK9 team member based in Santa Fe and hardly had the manpower to search for the suspect on his own. And at this point, aside from the MO and a few letters on the golden cuff link, he didn't have anything solid to tie the murdered John Doe to the RMK.

"I'd like you to take lead on questioning the party guests

and staff," Patricia added. "My priority right now is clearing the civilians and letting them get back to their homes and hotels. I'm hearing that they're all claiming they have an alibi for the shooting. But it's possible that somebody saw or heard something."

"I get that," Kyle said. He ran his hand over the back of his neck and felt the beginning of a sunburn. "But at the same time, something doesn't smell right about this."

The detective's dark eyes narrowed. "How so?"

"Let's say, hypothetically, our masked man lured our John Doe to the barn," Kyle said. "Maybe because this barn was close to where his victim lived or because he knew it would be hard for police to get to. Our killer stashes his car nearby to make a quick escape. Then he shoots John Doe in the chest and flees. On the surface, it looks like it matches the other RMK murders."

Patricia nodded.

"But there are discrepancies," Kyle said. "Why did he come back and keep shooting after the murder? CSI Clarke thought he was trying to destroy evidence. Did he realize he'd left something behind, see us go into the barn and try to stop us from getting our hands on it?"

"So you're saying that if it is your guy, maybe he's getting sloppy," Patricia said.

"Maybe," Kyle conceded.

And if so, what did that mean for the case? He couldn't even assume that the person who shot up the barn was also the man who killed John Doe.

Lord, guide Ophelia and the other crime scene investigators in gathering evidence. And guide me in questioning witnesses.

"I do have one thing for you," Patricia said. "One of the

CSI photographers got a good clear pic of the victim's face. I'll send it to you now."

She hit a couple of buttons on her phone and Kyle heard his own cell ping. He glanced down at the screen and got his first real, clear look at John Doe's face. The man was in his midtwenties and clean-shaven. That made him older than the RMK's first three victims, who'd been between the ages of nineteen and twenty-one, but younger than the most recent three who'd been in their late twenties and early thirties. His blond haircut looked expensive. So did his simple T-shirt. The victim definitely looked like the kind of guy who'd have been invited to the wedding.

Who are you, John Doe? And what were you doing here?

THREE

Kyle's feet itched to head back into the barn to check in with Ophelia and see if she'd discovered anything. Or even if she had any new theories. But instead, armed with as much info as Kyle could be for now, he and Rocky made their way to the ranch's main building to question the wedding party and potential witnesses. When he arrived, he was greeted by the cops at the door, who quickly briefed him on the investigation so far.

There were fifteen people who'd been there for the rehearsal party, including the bride and groom, four groomsmen, three bridesmaids, the groom's grandmother, his parents and three of the couple's friends. Then of course, Ophelia made sixteen, but obviously she wasn't being questioned. To his surprise, none of the bride's family was there, but apparently her parents had been flying in from overseas and their flight had been canceled due to a storm. The ranch staff consisted of two servers, a cook, a cleaner, the manager and two security guards.

So that made over twenty potential witnesses—or suspects.

It also turned out almost all of them had somebody else willing to vouch they'd been together when gunshots were fired. Only three people had nobody to back them up—the elderly cleaner, one of the security guards and the groom, Jared Clarke.

Kyle set himself up in a small lounge with low wooden tables and pale blue couches, and questioned each person, one by one in turn. Rocky lay by his feet and watched the proceedings.

Kyle verified where each person had been when the first set of gunshots sounded, and double-checked their answers matched the info the local police had already gathered. Then he showed them the picture of the victim and clocked their expressions. Thankfully, if anyone was nervous about talking to police, Rocky was an excellent icebreaker and thc hound was quick to make friends among the people Kyle questioned. But any hope Kyle had of gleaning something new from the witnesses was dashed, again and again, and nobody claimed to recognize John Doe, or had seen him before the shooting, or had any idea what he was doing at the ranch. And although most had heard of the Rocky Mountain Killer from social media or the news, all of them said they'd never been to Elk Valley, Wyoming or knew anyone who was a part of the Young Rancher's Club. Then one by one, he let them go, making sure he had their contact details on file and reminding them not to discuss the case with anyone and to keep their phones handy.

Everything was uneventful until he got to the groom, Jared. A few inches taller than Ophelia, with the same tanned skin, blond hair and blue eyes, he could be mistaken for her sibling, although he was her second cousin. Jared's tan suit and haircut were expensive. But they were coupled with the charisma of a damp sponge. He told Kyle he'd been alone at the time of the shooting. But he also claimed he didn't know or remember anything remotely helpful, and instead just waffled about how much he loved Gabrielle and needed the wedding to be perfect for her.

The whole endeavor was endlessly frustrating. His final interview was with the bride.

Gabrielle Martinez was about five-foot-two, with glossy black hair that both twisted around the crown of her head and fell in waves around her shoulders. Her dark eyes brimmed with worry. She plucked a candy from a bowl on the table and twisted the end of the wrapper back and forth, opening and closing it again.

"Are you sure that everyone is okay and that nobody else was hurt, Officer?" she asked.

"It's Agent, actually," he said, "and with the exception of our unknown victim nobody else was hurt."

She exhaled. "I'm so glad. They kind of ushered us in here and didn't tell us anything, or even let us talk to each other. Who was shot?"

"We haven't identified him yet," Kyle said. He slid his phone, with the picture open, toward her. "Do you recognize this man?"

"No." She shook her head.

"You sure you haven't seen him before?" Kyle pressed. "Take a good look."

Gabrielle stared down at the phone for a long moment. Then she shrugged.

"I'm so sorry," she said. "He might be one of Jared's colleagues from work. I know he invited a few I haven't met. But no, I've never seen him before in my life."

"Jared wasn't able to identify him, either," Kyle said.

He left his phone on the table and leaned back. How was

it possible a man showed up in the barn on the evening of a wedding rehearsal party and nobody knew who he was?

"And where were you when the shots were fired?"

"With Nolan Taft," Gabrielle said. "He's one of Jared's groomsmen. I'd just left Jared's grandmother in the suite where the bridesmaids would be getting dressed. Her name is Evelyn Clarke. Jared's cousin, Ophelia, had agreed to step in as a replacement bridesmaid because my friend Chloe Madison had canceled at the last minute and I was making sure Ophelia had everything she needed. When I left them, I went looking for Jared. I thought he might be at the outdoor, cliffside chapel where we're having our ceremony. I didn't see him there but I did bump into Nolan on the way back. We were talking about something, the weather I think, and then I heard the gunshots. We rushed toward the main building, and then ran into Jared. Then we heard a bunch of more shots."

Yeah, all this matched what other people had told him, too.

"Do you have any idea where your fiancé, Jared, was when the first gunshots sounded?"

Her eyes widened.

"No," she said. "He said he was looking for me. But I can't imagine Jared hurting anyone. He's the sweetest man I've ever known."

His grandmother had said the exact same thing. But if it did turn out the groom had something to do with this, he wouldn't be the first person to fool his loved ones about his true nature. And if Jared really was as bland and irritating as he appeared, that definitely didn't mean he couldn't also be a cold-blooded killer.

"How did you meet, Jared?" he asked. "I heard it was at a party."

"Yes, downtown Albuquerque," Gabrielle said, "about nine months ago. I was getting a degree in Design from the University of New Mexico, and my roommate Chloe and I went out to a networking party at this big hotel. But it was a really lame party, so we ended up going into the room where Jared's company was having a big dinner. He invited us to sit with him and we started talking. I guess you could say it was love at first sight." She glanced wistfully to the couch cushion beside her as if expecting to see him there. Then suddenly she gasped. Her hand rose to her lips. "Oh, please tell me that we can still get married tomorrow and we're not going to have to cancel the wedding!"

"It's not my call," Kyle said. "As for the ceremony itself, it's up to you and the venue. But even if you can't hold the wedding here, I'm sure your hotel or somewhere else will be able to accommodate you. And maybe a slight delay means your parents will make it in time. As for the investigation part of it, really, all that the police care about is figuring out who this John Doe is and who killed him." And despite his mild suspicions about Jared, he definitely didn't have cause to detain him, or anyone else, right now. "So, if you and your fiancé have nothing to do with that, you're free to go get married and live your lives."

He'd hoped his tone was reassuring. But the bride's frown only deepened.

"We just really had our heart set on getting married here," she said. "The mountains are really important to both of us and that barn was so perfect and pretty."

Well, now it's a murder scene. He imagined the bride

would dissolve into a puddle of tears if she saw just how badly her perfect reception venue had been destroyed.

"Considering the look in Jared's eyes when he told me about you, I'm sure he'd happily marry you in a grocery store parking lot," Kyle said in a kind tone. "I'm sure your wedding will still be beautiful and this is just a bump in the road on the way to your happily-ever-after."

Now that came out cornier than he'd hoped. But it seemed to work, because the bride was now smiling again.

"Can I go talk to Jared now?" she asked. "The cops wouldn't even let any of us sit together."

No doubt to make sure people weren't whispering back and forth coordinating their stories.

"Sure," he said. He stood. So did the bride. "I think we're done here for now. Just please don't discuss the case with anyone, including your fiancé."

Especially considering Jared was one of the few who didn't have an alibi for when John Doe was shot.

After Gabrielle left, he waited a few moments with Rocky, going over his sparse notes from the investigation so far and praying for wisdom. Then Kyle and his partner stepped out into the warm June night. To his right, he could see a trail of brake lights flickering as party guests and ranch staff made their way down the winding mountain road. There were fewer law enforcement vehicles in the parking lot now and police presence was a lot thinner on the grounds, too. He sent Chase a quick text telling him nothing concrete had been determined for now about the crime but that he looked forward to talking to him tomorrow.

He signaled Rocky to his side and walked back along the path to the barn to find a someone who could give him a ride back into Santa Fe. As they passed the courtyard,

Rocky's ears perked and his tail wagged, alerting Kyle to the fact that he'd found a friend. Then Kyle spotted her. Ophelia was standing by a low stone and clay wall, looking out over the waves of stars spreading up at the dark sky. Her blond hair was tied back in a ponytail and she'd changed from her purple dress into the standard-issue gray tracksuit and flip-flops that law enforcement kept on hand for victims needing a change of clothes.

Somehow she looked even more beautiful than she had before.

As if sensing his gaze, Ophelia turned toward them. A tired but gorgeous smile spread across her face. He felt an unfamiliar grin tug at the corner of his mouth.

He raised a palm up in greeting. "Hey."

"Hey, yourself." She started toward them. They stopped a few feet away from each other and stood in the courtyard, in a bright pool of light created by the glow of two different lamplights meeting. The smell of flowers, warm earth and pine filled the air. "Good news is that CSI is done processing the scene. Bad news is there's so much to go through and analyze it might take a couple of days. Plus, the lab is pretty backed up and understaffed. But I will do my best to expedite it when I'm in the lab tomorrow."

"Thanks," he said. "I'm especially curious about the cuff link. It's hard to imagine a serial killer going out and getting cuff links made with his moniker on them, but with the RMK you never know. A few weeks ago, he managed to get his hands on the MCK9 Task Force's compassion therapy labradoodle named Cowgirl. A few weeks ago, someone we believe to be the RMK sent our team leader, Chase Rawlston, a picture of Cowgirl from a burner phone, wearing a pink rhinestone dog collar that read Killer."

Her eyes widened. "Wow."

"Yeah," Kyle said. "Our technical analyst, Isla, is trying to track down where the collar was sold. But after pulling a stunt like that I wouldn't put getting gold cuff links with his moniker on them past the RMK. Did you find anything else interesting?"

"Well, personally, I think it's interesting we only found one cuff link," she said. "Considering they come in pairs. Did he leave one behind on purpose or by accident? But if you're looking for something more concrete, I can tell you the bullets were 9mm, if that means anything to you."

"Yeah, it really does." He blew out a hard breath. "Nine mm is the RMK's weapon of choice and all of the victims were killed with the same gun. I'll get Isla to coordinate with you tomorrow about seeing if you can confirm a match. The Mountain Country K-9 Task Force will be coordinating with the Santa Fe PD on this case for the time being."

"Guess that means we'll be working together," Ophelia said.

"We work together all the time," he said. "I just never knew that you were…you know, you. Or seen you outside of your protective gear."

"Probably for the best, considering the fact that the first time you did you ordered me out of your crime scene."

Her eyes twinkled. He could tell she was teasing him, but that didn't stop heat from rising to the back of Kyle's neck. He ran his hand over it.

"Sorry about that," he said. "The whole thing was kind of confusing, especially as we'd never really met and I didn't know why you'd requested me to respond to the scene."

To his surprise, a bright pink flush now spread across her cheeks.

"Well, dispatch told me that law enforcement was over twenty minutes out," she said, "and I knew that you were less than a quarter of a mile away."

That raised more questions than it answered. He waited, letting an uncomfortable pause lie between them as she struggled to find the words to explain.

"My great-aunt Evelyn is worried about me spending all my time with blood and death," she said, with a little laugh and a shrug, "so she created a profile for me on a dating app for elderly relatives who want to play matchmakers. She was showing it to me earlier and I recognized you from past cases we'd both worked on. It indicated you were really close by."

"Oh!" Kyle's heart stuttered a step. Someone had put him on a dating app. It had to be his mother. Yet, he'd have thought that if anyone knew that between his work with the MCK9 and being a dad to Brody he didn't have time to add a relationship into the mix, it would be her. Did she doubt his ability to be a good dad or think he was lacking in some way? Or was she worried that she wouldn't be able to be there for him forever? She'd definitely seemed distracted recently and did seem to need to drop by the drug store often these days, but whenever he'd asked her about it, she'd told him she was fine. "Yeah, I was actually at the petting zoo with my mother and son."

"I didn't know you had a son." Ophelia's eyes widened with what looked like genuine interest. "How old is he?"

"Eighteen months," Kyle said. He swallowed hard, feeling a familiar lump in his throat at the thought of how Brody had come into his life. No, he wouldn't burden her with all that. "Anyway, my mom lives with us. We also have a new puppy named Taffy, who's Rocky's half sister. It's a pretty busy house. I should probably say good-night, though. I need to see about finding a way back to town and I'm guessing you're heading out soon, too."

"Ophelia!" a man's voice called from the darkness.

They turned to see Jared running toward them. He looked worried.

"Jared!" Ophelia took a few steps toward him as he rushed toward them. "Is everything okay with Evelyn?"

"Yeah," he said. "A police officer has taken her and Gabrielle back to the hotel. Oh, and Grandma told me to tell you that she really hopes you decide to take that spare room, because you deserve to sleep in a luxury bed for a night. But there's something important that Gabrielle didn't tell you."

He glanced from Ophelia to Kyle and back, and Kyle had the distinct impression that whatever it was, Gabrielle didn't want Jared telling them now.

"Hey, you can trust Kyle," Ophelia said. "I've known him for a while and he's a great guy. One of the best."

Really? She thought that about him?

"Whatever's going on," she added, "you can trust us."

Jared glanced back over his shoulder. His voice lowered to a whisper.

"Gabrielle has a stalker," he said. "One who's been threatening to kill her."

"Gabrielle has a stalker?" Ophelia repeated.

She glanced at Kyle. His eyebrows rose as he met her gaze with a look that told her that this was the first he was hearing about it, too.

"Yeah," Jared said miserably. "His name is Bobby and

he's been harassing her for months, ever since he found out we were getting married."

"And neither of you ever went to the police with this?" Her voice rose. "You could've put her and everyone else at this wedding in danger."

"But we're thankful you're telling us now," Kyle told Jared, almost gently, as if he could read the frustration in her eyes. He gestured to a table with two stools that had been set up in the courtyard for the party that had never been. "Why don't we sit down and chat about it?"

Jared hesitated, then nodded. The three of them walked over to the table and Kyle pulled up a third stool. Rocky trotted over and sat down on the ground in between Kyle and Ophelia. The hound looked up at them and whimpered softly, as if sensing something was wrong and wondering if there was anything he could do to help. Ophelia leaned down and ran her hand over the back of Rocky's head as he nuzzled her fingers, comforting her even more than she was him.

Jared rested his elbows on the tiny table and dropped his head in his hands.

"This may not have anything to do with what happened," Jared said. Her cousin's gaze was locked on the table. "She told me it wasn't a big deal and I promised her I wasn't going to say anything." He looked so racked with guilt she felt her frustration with Jared begin to soften. "Is there any way we can keep this just between us?"

Not if it was related to a crime, Ophelia thought.

"I can keep this information within the immediate investigative team," Kyle said, "and only share it on a need-to-know basis. Trust me, people in my line of work get really adept at keeping other people's secrets. Nobody has to know about this conversation unless it becomes necessary for pressing charges and obtaining a conviction."

"Can we keep this out of the press?" Jared asked. "Gabrielle is really worried about this getting online or in the media, and I just really want to protect her."

"Absolutely," Kyle agreed. "Except in the event that it's needed as evidence for a trial."

Kyle was being so much kinder to Jared than she felt capable of being. To her, most things were cut-and-dried. As someone who collected and preserved evidence for a living, she was irked to no end by the fact that her cousin and Gabrielle had withheld potentially significant evidence from police. In her line of work things were binary. Either DNA was a match or it wasn't. Fingerprints had either been found at a crime scene or they hadn't been. There was something comforting about the certainty of that. But Kyle's tone was somehow multiple things at once. Both caring and firm. Not playing a good cop or bad cop, just a compassionate cop who also wouldn't flinch from seeking justice.

Jared paused for a moment. Then he sighed and crossed both arms on the table.

"Yeah, I guess that's fair," he said. "Gabrielle just comes from a very wealthy and very private family who are worried about her reputation. So she has to be really careful about avoiding scandals or anything that will damage their image. They're really old-fashioned and she's worried about getting disowned if she's caught up in some kind of scandal."

Ophelia wondered if that had anything to do with Great-Aunt Evelyn's earlier implication that there was some kind of tension with Gabrielle's parents missing their flight and Jared needing help dealing with some problem related to the venue. Did they think Jared wasn't good enough for their daughter?

"Yeah, I hear you," Kyle said, "and I get that."

"So, you know how I told you that we met at a party in a hotel in Albuquerque last September? Well, Gabrielle and her roommate Chloe had gone to this other party first, with some students from her college, and this guy named Bobby had shown up."

"Was he also a college student?" Kyle interjected.

"No," Jared said. "He was some kind of investments guy from Nevada, who made money in online currencies. They'd only gone on a couple of dates and he'd gotten really demanding. Anyway, I was there at a table with a bunch of my colleagues when she came in and asked if she could hide out at my table and sit with me until the guy gave up and stopped looking for her. We got talking, I offered to walk her home, and next thing I knew we'd spent hours just wandering the city getting to know each other."

Despite the worry that lined his forehead, a smile filled his eyes at the memory.

"Where was Chloe at this time?" Kyle asked. "She's the bridesmaid that didn't show up, right?"

"I don't know." Jared frowned. "She made herself scarce shortly after Gabrielle and I started talking. I was honestly so caught up in Gabrielle I didn't notice. I know Gabrielle was devastated when Chloe canceled on her today." He glanced at Ophelia. "By the way, I haven't forgotten that I told you I wouldn't try to rope you in to be a bridesmaid, but it was kind of an emergency."

Ophelia bit her tongue and stopped herself from pointing out he and Gabrielle had an odd definition of what constituted an "emergency."

"Was it love at first sight?" Kyle asked.

Jared nodded. "Yeah, absolutely, I'd never met anyone like her."

"Did you see Bobby that night?" Kyle asked.

"No, I've never seen him," Jared said. "I have noticed a large guy in a hoodie who seemed to be lurking around her apartment or following us sometimes, but I never got a good look at him. And I didn't even know if it was him. At times I thought maybe I was being paranoid."

"Did she tell you about Bobby that night you met?" Kyle pressed.

"Absolutely," Jared said. "She told me right away that someone was hassling her and I didn't really ask her for the details. I was just happy to help her."

"But you didn't realize it was a problem?"

"Not for a couple of weeks," Jared said. "We'd gone out for dinner and when I dropped her off there was this big bouquet of flowers outside her apartment door. Absolutely huge. She got all flustered and upset and told me that Bobby was fixated on her and had somehow figured out where she lived. He was really relentless, refusing to take no for an answer."

"And did you suggest she go to the police?" Kyle asked.

"Of course! But she didn't want to because she has a really big heart and I think she felt sorry for the guy."

"And because of her wealthy and controlling parents, right?" Kyle suggested.

The fact that Jared had given two different explanations for the why they'd chosen not to go to the police about Gabrielle's stalker didn't mean there wasn't some truth to both of them. But it did make her wonder if Gabrielle and Jared had been lying to themselves about how potentially serious the situation was.

"Yeah," Jared said. "I feel weird talking to a cop about this, but apparently Bobby was really well connected in law enforcement and he told Gabrielle if she called the police on him they wouldn't do anything to protect her from him." He glanced at Ophelia again. "I think it would help a lot if you assured her that you and Kyle are friends, and that you can promise us that Kyle's got our back and is on our side."

She felt her lips beginning to part to tell Jared she'd do no such thing, when she saw Kyle subtly wave his hand, a couple of inches above the table, signaling to her to let the comment go.

"Does she know Bobby's last name? Where he lives and where he works?"

"No, just his first name."

"Hmm." Kyle leaned back and crossed his arms. "Not a lot to go on, then. Were the flowers a onetime thing?"

"No, there were phone calls, too, day and night, from different blocked numbers. He also left notes on her door sometimes, which is how I know he said that he'd kill her if she married me, and if he couldn't have her nobody could."

"There are notes?" Ophelia asked. "Where are they now? We can do handwriting analysis, track where the paper came from and test them for fingerprints and DNA."

"Sadly, she burned them all," Jared said. "She just wanted to erase him from her life. It's part of why we decided to get married in Santa Fe instead of Albuquerque. She just wanted to put him behind her and move on."

Only maybe the danger had followed them here.

"And you wanted to be her knight in shining armor and protect her," Kyle said.

"Yeah."

Ophelia sat and listened for another fifteen minutes or so as Jared spoke and Kyle asked insightful questions. But it was clear they were just talking around in circles and Jared had told him everything he knew.

Finally, Kyle reached over and placed a comforting hand on Jared's forearm.

"It's clear that you love her a lot," he said. "And you're really worried for her. You should head back to the hotel and go be with her." Then Kyle stood as if to signal the conversation was over. So did Jared and Ophelia. "I suggest you tell her that you told us about this Bobby guy and encourage her to talk to us about him. You can both sleep on it, and maybe she'll be willing to talk to us tomorrow and fill in some of the gaps. Tell her that it could really go a long way in helping with our investigation. But either way, I will do everything in my power to unravel what happened here today and keep you guys safe, okay?"

"Okay," Jared said. He still seemed a bit shaky, but lighter, too, as if he'd managed to get a weight off his shoulders. He hugged Ophelia and she hugged him back. "I don't think I'm going to be able to get her to talk to police. But maybe I can get her to talk to you, Ophelia. Because you're family and she seems to really like you. I'll just explain that Kyle's an FBI agent friend of yours and on our side."

Again, she could see Kyle's warning gaze on her face telling her to let the comment slide. So she just pressed her lips together and wished Jared a good night. She stood back with Kyle and Rocky, and watched her cousin saunter to the parking lot.

Kyle pulled his phone from his pocket, glanced at the screen and frowned.

"Everything okay?" Ophelia asked.

"Yeah," Kyle said. "Well, no, actually. I missed Brody's bedtime. My mom usually does his morning routine and I do nighttime. He's fussing that he doesn't want to go to sleep without saying good-night to Rocky and me." He glanced down at his dog. Rocky thumped his tail on the ground. "I'm sure the one he really wants to see is Rocky. He really loves my partner."

"Well, Rocky's a very lovable dog," she agreed.

The hound woofed as if thanking her for the compliment. She laughed.

"Problem is we all came to the petting zoo together in my vehicle," he said, "and I had her take it back. I told her I'd get a ride home with one of the cops on the scene, but most of them have left by now. And I don't know how long it's going to take to get a taxi up here."

"I'll give you a ride," Ophelia said quickly.

"You sure?"

"Of course, I don't mind. It'll give us time to talk." His gaze was unreadable as she added, "About the case."

He nodded. She wished she could spend the time learning more about him and the family he seemed devoted to. Despite the work on her PhD she knew she needed to get home to, somehow she wasn't quite ready for the evening to end. And maybe neither was he. Because another look she couldn't quite decipher flickered in Kyle's eyes, one that seemed to draw her closer while also sending a fresh wave of heat rising to her cheeks. She broke his gaze and looked down at Rocky.

"Although obviously the one I really want to talk to is Rocky."

Kyle snorted a laugh. "Obviously."

He fired off a couple of quick texts as they walked to the almost empty parking lot.

"Mine's the little one," she said.

She pressed a button on her remote and her small car unlocked and flashed its lights in greeting. She opened the back door for Rocky, who leaped inside and positioned himself in the middle, in between her gym bag, a box of spare plastic gloves and some of her research books. Kyle opened the passenger door and slid the seat all the way back, before folding his tall frame inside. She got in the driver's seat and was instinctively about to apologize for having such a modest car, instead of the fancier ones the other wedding guests had, before realizing that for once she was sitting beside someone who already knew what she did for a living, understood what it entailed and even relied on it.

It was a nice feeling.

She glanced to the rearview mirror and saw Rocky's cheerful face smiling back at her, as if riding in her small and crowded car was some kind of grand adventure. She smiled and pulled out.

Slowly, they drove back through the wedding arch, out of the ranch and down the steep, narrow and winding mountain road. A drive that had seemed a bit tricky during the evening felt almost treacherous now.

"I didn't know you had a family," she admitted. She had happened to notice he didn't wear a wedding ring. But that kind of routine observation was a hazard of the job.

"When my fraternal twin and his wife died in a helicopter crash in the mountains last year, their six-month-old son, Brody, was orphaned. And I adopted my nephew."

"Oh, I'm so sorry for your loss." She clenched the steering wheel to keep from squeezing his hand reassuringly.

How awful for him. "I remember hearing about the accident. I didn't realize that was your family. What was your twin like?"

"Kevin was perfect. At least in my eyes. He was confident and always seemed so certain of both himself and God. He just threw himself into everything without hesitation. I admired him so much. I always wished I was more like him, and then he was gone, and it felt like I'd lost the person who inspired me most." He ran his hand through his dark hair. "I don't think I ever admitted that to anyone before."

She swerved the car around a blind corner. Suddenly a white delivery van loomed ahead, parked at the side of the road. She turned the wheel sharply and barely managed not to clip it. *Thank You, God, that I wasn't driving faster.* She guessed somebody had picked an inopportune place to stop and stargaze. The van's headlights flickered on and then off again. Kyle glanced at it over his shoulder for a long moment, then turned back.

"I need to ask you something about Jared," Kyle said. "Are you two close?"

"Yes," she said automatically. "Well, to a point. We grew up together. My grandmother passed away when I was little, and his grandmother, my great-aunt Evelyn, really stepped in to take her place. I spent every holiday with Evelyn and Jared. My parents are both university professors who traveled a lot for work. But honestly, I wouldn't say Jared and I are close, as people."

Something about how candid he was about Kevin made her want to be honest, too.

"We're both only children and I used to assume we were close," she went. "But our personalities are really different.

He's not the kind of person who stops to question how he comes across to other people."

"And how does he come across?" Kyle asked.

"I don't know how to put it," she said. "Self-centered, maybe? I'd almost say he was spoiled but that sounds too childish. Or privileged, but that word is too easily misinterpreted."

"What was your first job?" Kyle asked.

She blinked. "How is that relevant?"

"Hey, you focus on gathering evidence and I do the interpreting, remember?"

There was a grin in his voice. Yeah, she remembered telling him that back at the barn.

"I was a waitress all through high school," she said.

"And Jared's first job?"

"A friend of his dad's got him a position at his firm after college."

Headlights appeared in the rearview mirror. She turned another corner and they vanished again.

"When you and Jared visited Evelyn, was he expected to clear the table and do his own dishes?"

"No," she said.

"How about picking his clothes up off the floor?"

"No, those were my jobs," Ophelia said. "Evelyn had pretty strong opinions about gender roles, and whenever I complained she'd say Jared had the responsibility of protecting the family if we ever went to war."

To her surprise, Kyle chuckled under his breath.

"Sorry, I'm just imagining ten-year-old Ophelia standing over a sink full of dirty dishes wondering when exactly the invading armies were going to arrive."

She giggled, despite herself. Her great-aunt was certainly grounded in her opinions about women's roles, but she'd always made Ophelia feel welcome in her home. She knew Evelyn loved her. Ophelia just wished her aunt had understood how some of her comments made her feel.

"That's not far off," she said. "And you can't have missed Jared assuming that because we know each other, you'd be 'his cop' and on his side."

"No, I didn't," Kyle said dryly.

"Truth is my parents were really big on personal responsibility," she said. "Jared had it a lot easier and his side of the family was a lot wealthier than mine. Although Evelyn did say something about a plot of land Gabrielle's parents are buying for them that made me wonder if there were money problems."

"What plot of land?" Kyle interjected.

"A gorgeous place near the Pecos Wilderness that they're going to build a house on," Ophelia said. "Jared was so ostentatious about it. Said they'd decided to build a house 'where the mountains meet the sky,' et cetera. It was so pompous."

"Not cheap," Kyle said.

"No," Ophelia agreed. "Plus, this whole wedding has been expensive and exorbitant. So maybe he's been overspending. But please, don't get me wrong, they're not bad people. And even if I did end up doing a lot more housework than Jared did, I know Evelyn loves me and she would've been the first person to tell Jared to go mow the lawn and chop wood, if she hadn't had a gardener and central heating."

Kyle chuckled. Then his smile dropped almost immediately, as headlights reappeared on their tail.

"Do me a favor," he said, "and turn left at this next fork."

"Will do." She focused on keeping the pace steady as the turn ahead grew closer. Then at the last possible moment she tapped her brakes just enough to safely pull off the road that would've led them back to the highway in a matter of minutes and onto one that would take them on a longer route past hiking trails. The van kept going forward.

Kyle leaned back against the seat.

"Do you think you're able to be impartial if the evidence points to your cousin?" he asked.

"I don't think he's capable of hurting anyone."

"His fiancée and grandmother agree with you on that," Kyle said. "But the fact is that Jared had no alibi for when John Doe was killed. Now, our victim was tall and blond like your cousin. It's possible Bobby was gunning for Jared and shot John Doe by mistake. But I also have to consider that the victim *is* Bobby, that he came here to stop the wedding and Jared shot him to protect Gabrielle."

"But then who was the man who shot into the barn?" Ophelia asked. "Because that can't have been Jared."

"I don't know."

The road seemed to stretch out endlessly in front of them. The lights of Santa Fe grew closer. Eventually ranch houses began to appear, up and down the mountain on either side. She felt like she was standing on the edge of something very tall and he was asking her to be willing to jump.

Lord, help me keep an open mind about this. Don't let my feelings blind my vision.

"Okay," she said finally. "I can promise you I'll do my job, gather the evidence, process it impartially and trust you to draw your own conclusions."

Which didn't mean she'd necessarily agree with him.

Only that she knew she was probably unconsciously biased toward her cousin and would try to keep an open mind.

After all, Kyle would be the one who'd make the call on whether any charges would be laid. And she wouldn't get in the way of him doing his job.

"Good." Kyle let out a long breath. "Because Jared seems willing to tell you things that he won't tell me."

Kyle's gaze darted up to the rearview mirror and her gaze followed. The headlights had returned.

"Also, I may be wrong," he said. "But I think we're being followed."

FOUR

The glare of the twin headlights filled Ophelia's rearview mirror. Fear trickled down her spine. Was it the same van? Was it really following them? She couldn't even imagine how hard it would've been for a van like that to have done a U-turn on the steep mountain road to turn around and get after them again.

She spotted a residential neighborhood ahead to her right. Instinctively, she turned in through the gate and weaved her way through the houses, before coming back to the same road she'd been on before, hoping the van wouldn't follow and Kyle would turn out to be mistaken. But instead, the van followed every move.

The sense of dread grew deeper. She gripped the steering wheel so tightly her hand shook.

Help me, Lord. I don't know who this guy is or what he wants, but please keep us safe.

"You're right," she said. "I'm sorry, I just wanted to double-check."

"I respect that," Kyle said.

"So, what do we do?" she asked.

He glanced back at the van over his shoulder. "I can't get a good look at the guy and his license plate is too dirty to read. And I don't want to risk getting into a high-speed chase with the guy."

Neither did she. She had to force her eyes to stay on the road ahead and not keep glancing to the headlights on her tail. Kyle turned to Rocky and ordered him to get onto the floor and lie down. The K-9 woofed in agreement and complied. Then Kyle sat back in his seat.

"I'm sorry," he said, "I just realized I didn't think to ask if you do have any training or experience in tactical driving."

A laugh slipped through her lips. Not because the situation was funny. But because she was so used to being underestimated she couldn't actually remember the last time anyone overestimated her.

"Not in the slightest," she said. "If you need someone to gather DNA samples or process crime scene evidence I'm your gal. But anything that involves high-speed chases or action scenes is out of my wheelhouse."

She watched as his jaw set in determination.

"Well, if I could find a safe way to pull over and change places with you I would," he said. "But I don't want to risk it."

He paused for a long moment and when she glanced his way she noticed his eyes were closed and he seemed to be praying. She echoed his prayers, asking God to hear his plea.

Then Kyle opened his eyes again.

"Okay," he said. "I want you to head to downtown Santa Fe. I want to get this guy into the light and get a good look at who we're dealing with."

Another fork in the road appeared ahead. This time she turned toward the city. Santa Fe, the capital of New Mexico, was nestled in the foothills of the Rocky Mountains. The road sloped steeply beneath her tires. The beautiful lights of the city dazzled below her like dozens of tiny tea light candles floating on the surface of a lake.

The vehicle behind turned and followed. It was stalking them like an animal, not driving close enough to run them off the road and yet never getting too far from sight, no matter how many twists and turns she took. The city grew closer; ranches and houses gave way to densely packed roads dotted with stop signs and traffic lights.

As the warm glow of Santa Fe surrounded them, she could see the van pull back as if shirking from the light. But finally, they were able to get a good look at the van. It was an old delivery vehicle, with no windows or obvious markings on the side. The kind someone could buy from a used car dealership or steal from a small business lot. She couldn't see much of the man who was behind the wheel. He was hunched low and wearing a baseball cap. Traffic continued to slow. Black and yellow signs advertising road closures appeared ahead. Summer weekends in Santa Fe were a rolling feast of events and festivals, celebrating New Mexico's culture, diversity, music, agriculture and cuisine. The sound of string instruments and singing filled the air.

"Keep going," Kyle said, "right up to the barriers. We're looking for a road that's been blocked off by police. I'll get them to wave us in through the barrier and then surround the van before he can turn around again."

Kyle raised his phone to his ear, called dispatch and briefed them on his location and plan.

"We need a tight perimeter," he said. "Consider the suspect armed and dangerous. He's a possible suspect in a string of murders across several states."

But the words had barely left his lips when she glanced

to the rearview mirror to see the van turn sharply, mount the sidewalk and pull down a side road.

Kyle sighed and updated dispatch of the van's new route.

"Do you want me to turn around and go after him?" Ophelia asked.

"Nah." Kyle sounded frustrated. "Last thing I want to do is get in a chase with a suspect who might be armed in a public place." After he ended his call with dispatch, he placed a very quick call to Chase, the leader of the MCK9 Task Force, and quickly briefed him on the night so far.

"We have a video chat first thing tomorrow morning," he told Ophelia when he finished the call. "We'll go over things more thoroughly then. One piece of very good news is that he's going to ask Meadow Ames to join us on the call and potentially fly out to back me up on this case, depending on how things go. She's a US marshal and an incredible member of our team. Her K-9 partner, Grace, is a vizsla who specializes in search and rescue." The relief in his voice was palpable. "Are you good?"

"Yep," she said. "I'm just driving in circles right now, waiting for direction."

He chuckled. There was something warm about it, like he appreciated her company. He rattled off his home address and she laughed. Turned out they lived in the same neighborhood on the north side of the city.

"My house is a fifteen-minute walk from yours," she said. "I'm just on Chestnut Street."

"Awesome." He turned and told Rocky he could get back up on the seat. Rocky woofed joyfully and hopped onto the back seat. A moment later the dog's cheerful face appeared in the rearview mirror again.

She waved a hand. "Hi, Rocky!"

He woofed again in greeting and she laughed.

"I've met a lot of K-9 dogs in my line of work," she said, "but Rocky is one of a kind. There's a real gentleness to him. I don't know if it's those long floppy ears or if the beige muzzle and paws make it look like he's been playing in chocolate milk, but there's a sweetness to him."

"Yeah," Kyle said. "I didn't know what to think when I was paired with a cadaver dog. It felt like such a sad specialty. But as I started working with him, I really came to appreciate his dedication and focus, along with how our work brings peace and justice to families who've lost their loved ones."

"That's really beautiful," she said, "and kind of poetic."

"Nobody's ever called me a poet before."

Something sizzled inside her chest, like a dozen party sparklers springing to life.

"Well, nobody's ever asked me if I'm a stunt driver before," she said.

He laughed again, this time a full-throated chuckle that seemed to come from somewhere deep inside his chest.

"I like hanging with you, CSI Clarke," he said. He punched her shoulder gently, as if they were siblings. "You're a pal. This is a really hard job sometimes and people like you make it easier."

"Thanks, Agent West." Not that she was sure what to make of the fact that he'd just fist-bumped her shoulder and called her "pal."

She liked hanging with him, too. Even though her body ached for sleep, something inside her wasn't ready for the car ride to end. But all too soon, GPS alerted her that her destination was ahead on the right, and she looked up to see a large, ranch-style house with Kyle's vehicle and a smaller red car parked out front. She pulled in.

Through a window, she could see the silhouette of a woman with long hair swaying with a toddler in her arms, as if trying to get him to settle.

"Well, I should get going," he said. "Looks like my mom hasn't managed to get Brody down yet. He's a really good kid, most of the time. But he gets stubborn when he doesn't want to sleep. Thanks again for the ride."

"No problem," she said. "Have a good night."

"You, too," he said.

Yet he didn't reach for the door handle. She didn't move, either. Instead, they both sat there, smiling at each other.

"Again, I'm sorry that in all the cases we've both worked I never took the time to come over to introduce myself," he said. "I've always really admired your work. Your job is a rough one and you do it well."

"You have no idea what that means to me," she said. "I admire your work, too. My great-aunt Evelyn actually told me not to talk about my job at the wedding. 'Nobody wants to hear about murder and crime scenes. It's impolite.'" She wagged her finger in an impression of Evelyn. He laughed. "And apparently Gabrielle thought I was some kind of veterinarian, because on top of my job with the crime lab, I'm also pursuing a PhD in using DNA to track the endangered Rocky Mountain wolf population."

"That's absolutely incredible," he said. "Considering the hours we work I can't imagine juggling the job and a PhD."

"It's a lot," she admitted. "I feel like I'm never getting enough sleep and sometimes I forget to eat. But I can't imagine juggling the job and single parenthood. At least

I only have to worry about me. You have Brody to worry about."

"Yeah, being his dad on top of work doesn't leave much time for anything else," he said. "Which reminds me, I have to ask my mom about that dating profile you saw and get her to take it down. The last thing I want is to fool some poor woman into thinking I'm free for a relationship right now."

And just like that, the sparklers she'd felt inside her chest went out as suddenly as if he'd dumped a bucket of cold water on them. He wasn't directing that comment at her. Of course. Kyle thought of her as a work pal and was only speaking his truth. He had no idea that she was attracted to him. And besides, it wasn't like she was looking for a relationship, either. They both had busy and demanding full-time jobs, on top of her PhD and the fact that he was raising a toddler.

Neither of them had time for anything more.

No matter how many fireworks his smile set off inside her chest.

"You should probably delete your dating profile, too," Kyle said. His dark eyes searched her face and a question hung in their gaze. "Unless you want to be on a website like that."

"Yeah, no," Ophelia said. "You're right. I should totally delete that profile."

Kyle nodded. "We should exchange numbers, to follow up with each other about the case. If that's all right with you."

"Absolutely." For professional reasons and nothing else. No other reason.

They exchanged numbers. Then she leaned in between the seats, ran her hand over Rocky's head and wished him a good night. Rocky woofed softly and licked her hand.

Kyle got out of the car and called for his partner, and she watched them both walk toward the house.

There was something so sweet about them. They were solid and comforting. She felt safe around them, like she knew they'd do what it took to bring criminals to justice.

She closed her eyes and prayed.

Lord, please help us find the identity of the John Doe who died in the barn and catch his killer. Help me focus on the evidence in front of me. Help me do my job without getting distracted by my emotions. Remind me that You called me to this work for a reason and help me trust in You.

Then she prayed that God would bless Kyle and his family, along with Jared, his fiancée, Gabrielle, her great-aunt Evelyn, the other venue staff, law enforcement and all those impacted by the murder in the barn, and those who loved the victim.

She hadn't meant to sit in Kyle's driveway praying that long, but when she opened her eyes, she looked to see Kyle silhouetted in the same window where she'd seen his mother earlier, gently dancing around the room with the small boy in his arms. The FBI agent bent low over the boy, like he was brushing a kiss on the toddler's head or whispering in his ear.

Her breath caught in her throat; it was like she was looking at a picture of something she'd never let herself acknowledge she wanted for herself one day, because she knew she'd never find it.

Slowly she pulled out of the driveway and drove home. Ophelia lived in a small stucco bungalow that sat by itself at the end of a dead-end road, with an empty lot on one side and building under construction on the other. It had a perfectly square living room, a surprisingly large kitchen, a single bedroom in the back and a small, unfinished basement. She dropped her bag on the table beside her front door and then walked through the living room and into the bedroom, tossing the remains of the purple bridesmaid dress into her closet hamper.

Her phone battery was almost dead, so she plugged her phone into a charger by the front door and placed a quick call to Evelyn. Her great-aunt assured her that she was fine and that "a lovely hotel manager" had promised her personally that his security would keep a close eye on the hotel. Ophelia told Evelyn that she loved her, wished her a good night and ended the call quickly before she could get trapped in a longer conversation.

Ophelia knew she should probably eat, considering she'd never ended up having dinner, and should also get some sleep. But something inside her just couldn't settle. Did her cousin have something to do with John Doe's murder? Had the man who'd shot at her been the Rocky Mountain Killer? What would she find when she processed the evidence?

Either way, she had to read at least twenty-five pages before bed if she had any hope of meeting her next deadline with her PhD advisor. Ophelia sat on the bed, tucked her feet beneath her quilt, pulled out one of her heavy research books and tried to get through the reading. She spun a pencil between her fingers, underlining anything she thought might be useful to follow up on her thesis and jotted notes in the margins, until finally she fell asleep with her book on her chest.

Ophelia woke up to a dark house and a gnawing in her stomach that told her she'd forgotten to eat. She reached for her lamp and toggled the switch back and forth, but the room stayed dark. She walked into the main room to find the light switch there didn't work, either, and the cell phone she'd left plugged in was completely dead.

Okay, looked like the power was out. One of the downsides of living in a hot state during the summer months was that sometimes everyone turned their air-conditioning on at once, causing brownouts.

All the more reason to get something to eat from the fridge before the food spoiled. She headed through the quiet, dark house to the kitchen, still in the same tracksuit she'd been wearing since the crime scene. A faint and foul smell hung in the air and she wondered if her food had already begun to spoil. The fridge was off, but when she pulled a carton of chocolate ice cream from the freezer she was thankful to find it wasn't too melted. She leaned over the counter and ate it straight from a carton with a spoon.

Her gaze flickered to where she'd left her laptop on the kitchen table. She still hadn't looked at the dating profile her aunt had set up for her on Loving Meddlers. And even though she knew that reading whatever Great-Aunt Evelyn had posted in her profile wasn't going to help her get back to sleep, she was curious. She opened her laptop and searched for the website. The gentle glow of the screen filled the kitchen.

The site opened quickly. It had a bubblegum pink background and photos of happy couples. Much smaller text warned users not to create profiles for their single loved ones without their permission and had a button to click for people to remove a profile that somebody had made about them. A pop-up window on the side told her that Kyle's profile had recently checked out hers and gave her the opportunity to contact him now by video chat.

A couple of clicks later, the profile her great-aunt had created for her showed up.

Ophelia sighed, feeling the ice cream turn to ash in her mouth. There was nothing actually wrong with the profile. It was sweet, actually, with a picture of her smiling in a sundress at her aunt's seventieth birthday garden party. It described her as charming, pretty, generous and kind. But there was nothing listed about her education, work or goals. Nothing about the accomplishments she was proud of or what she liked about herself.

No man wants to marry a woman who pokes around blood and guts for a living.

A thud sounded from somewhere beneath her feet. She froze. Was there something in the basement? Then she heard the telltale sound of footsteps creaking on the basement stairs. Someone was climbing up the stairs, one by one, toward her. Her heart pounded hard in her chest, blocking her ability to breathe. Her phone was dead. Should she run? Or hide? If she tried to dash for the front door, she'd have to first pass the basement to get there. Would she make it in time?

No. The footsteps had almost reached the top of the stairs. She snatched up the laptop and dove beneath the table. She needed to call for help. But how? She had no way to call 911. And while she could contact Santa Fe PD via the internet, she'd have to hurry to get to the site and there was no time. The basement door handle was already beginning to turn. The dating website's ridiculous message box flashed.

She held her breath, prayed and hit the button. The heart-shaped icon spun. The call went unanswered. She heard the creek of hinges as the basement door swung open. Footsteps sounded on her living room floor. Ophelia typed her address rapid fire into the chat box and told Kyle she needed help, that there was someone in her home.

"Hello?" A woman's face appeared on the screen. She had long gray hair and worried eyes. "Ophelia? I'm Alice, Kyle's mom. Are you okay?"

Footsteps pounded toward her.

"I need help!" Ophelia yelled. "There's someone in my home—"

But it was too late. The table that she'd been hiding under suddenly flipped over, clattering on the floor beside her. Large, gloved hands grabbed her by the hair and yanked her whimpering to her feet.

"Now, what are you doing here?" The man's voice was harsh and angry. His face was hidden in the same mask she'd seen before, with a dark mesh that even hid his eyes. For a split second she could see Alice's panicked face looking up at her. Then he kicked the laptop hard, shattering the screen and sending it flying.

Leaving Ophelia alone with her attacker.

"Kyle!" his mother's voice shouted. "Someone named Ophelia is in trouble!"

Kyle jerked awake as Brody's bedroom door swung open. He'd fallen asleep on a mattress on the floor of Brody's room, holding the little boy's hand through the crib, with both Rocky and Taffy curled up beside him. He fell asleep there most nights, gazing into Brody's face and listening to the child's tiny breath rise and fall.

Kyle leaped to his feet and rushed out to the hallway with both dogs on his heels before his brain had even fully computed what his mother was saying. Questions cascaded through his mind, like how she would even know that, but only one truly mattered.

"Is Ophelia okay?"

"No." Alice closed Brody's door. Her voice was an urgent whisper. "A man broke into her home and grabbed her."

"When?"

"Thirty seconds ago, maybe."

That was all he needed to know.

He ran for the front door, summoning Rocky to his side. "She lives on Chestnut. Do you know where?"

"Number 32," Alice said. "She messaged me on this dating app I set up for you. Should I call 911?"

"Yes," Kyle said. "But I'm not going to wait for them."

He just prayed to the Lord that he'd make it in time. Kyle grabbed his badge and gun, shoved his feet into his shoes and dashed out the front door with Rocky at his heels. His mother barely managed to grab Taffy and scoop her up into her arms before the puppy could run out after them.

He glanced at his truck, mapped the route out in his mind and made the split-second decision he could get there faster on foot.

"Come on, Rocky!" he yelled. "We're going to make a run for it!"

His feet raced down the sidewalk with his partner keeping pace. Desperate prayers poured through his heart, begging God to keep her alive and safe until he could get there.

A swing set loomed ahead in the distance. He turned toward it and cut through the park, racing past the jungle gym and slide. A six-foot wooden fence appeared ahead.

"Rocky!" he called to his partner. "Jump!"

Kyle leaped up the fence. His toes catching the wood part way up, he braced his hands against the top of the fence and vaulted over. Then he glanced back and watched as Rocky cleared it in a single bound. He crossed another street, then ran up a driveway and cut through a stranger's backyard, praying for the peaceful sleep of those inside. They scaled another fence and came out on Chestnut Street. He gasped for breath and scanned house numbers.

Rocky growled and signaled to his right to where a house sat all alone at the end of the street. The lights were off. A white van was parked on the side of the road in front of number 32. As Kyle ran for it, his partner barked, and Kyle felt his heart lurch in response. The warning sound was unmistakable.

Rocky sensed death.

No! The single word detonated like a bomb in Kyle's heart. Rocky had to be wrong for once. Kyle couldn't have lost her. Something deep inside his core needed her to be alive. They reached the house and ran up the driveway. Rocky's nose sniffed the air and growled.

But Kyle could now hear the sounds of a struggle coming from inside the house. A second later he was at the door. It was locked. Kyle reared back and leveled a swift kick just below the doorknob, and it flew open.

"Agent Kyle West!" He burst through into the living room. "FBI!"

His eyes adjusted to the darkness. The same masked man whom Kyle had chased through the mountains had Ophelia around the throat, even as she tried to thrash and fight against him. A thick cloth he'd tied around his left calf over his pant leg was caked in dried blood. The man dragged her backward toward an open doorway, limping heavily. His left arm tightened cruelly around her neck as he pulled her in front of him like a human shield. Metal glinted in his right hand. A gun? A knife?

Rocky barked wildly, held back only by the fact that Kyle hadn't given him the order to leap.

"Let her go!" Kyle raised his weapon and set the masked man in his sights. But he couldn't get a clean shot.

Help me, Lord. I can't risk firing and hurting Ophelia!

FIVE

"Turn around and leave!" The masked man's shout was followed by a string of vile swear words and threats of what he'd do to Ophelia if Kyle didn't retreat.

There was no way he was going to let that happen.

Rocky snarled. The man yanked Ophelia back harder toward the door, and his arm slipped up in front of Ophelia's face. She grabbed it and bit down hard. Her attacker shouted in pain and instinctively shoved her away hard.

Ophelia flew at Kyle, barely giving him seconds to sheath his weapon before she crashed into him. He caught her and held her tightly to his side. Her weight fell into his arms as her legs collapsed out from under her.

The assailant pushed past them, bodychecking Kyle so violently he almost knocked him off his feet, and ran out the front door. Rocky barked sharply.

"I'm fine." Ophelia's voice shook even as he could tell she was trying to regain control of it. "Go after him!"

Even in the darkness he could see the tears filling the blue of her eyes.

The memory of the second set of gunshots back at the barn rattled in his mind. How could he leave her now? The criminal knew where she lived and had invaded her home.

What if he had an accomplice hiding nearby waiting for Kyle to leave so he could make another attempt to kidnap Ophelia when she was alone and helpless?

Kyle couldn't have hesitated more than a few seconds, before relinquishing his grip on Ophelia's quivering frame. Then he made sure her feet were stable on the floor and pulled his weapon.

"Stay behind me and keep low," he told Ophelia. She nodded.

He signaled Rocky to his side and then he cautiously stepped out into the warm June night, just in time to hear the van door slam. The white van peeled away down the street.

Kyle pivoted quickly and ran for Ophelia's car, with Rocky just two steps behind. Instinctively, he glanced to Ophelia's car as he debated going after him. Both of her back tires were slashed. The white van's taillights disappeared around a corner.

Kyle groaned.

"Bad news," he called. "You've got two flats."

Ophelia sighed loudly and Rocky whimpered softly as if asking Kyle how he could help. Kyle ran his hand over the back of his partner's neck.

"I'm sorry," Ophelia said. She clenched her fingers around her keys. "I wish I'd found a way to contact you sooner, or somehow found a way to stop him, or get the better of him, or..."

"Stop it." Kyle stepped toward her and her words trailed off. "*None* of this is your fault in the slightest. You did nothing wrong."

He ran his hand over his head and realized that as much

as he wanted to kick himself, it wouldn't do either of them much good.

"You got help, you stayed alive and survived." Kyle's voice dropped, remembering how she'd been trembling in his arms. "Sometimes that's all you can do and it's more than enough."

She nodded and he watched as her chin rose.

"What happened to your phone?" he asked.

"The battery was dead when I woke up," she said. "The power is out."

Yeah, the lights had been off when he'd run up and he hadn't tried to turn them on.

"Okay," he said. "So you've got no power and two flat tires. I'm guessing whoever our attacker is, he didn't want you getting away."

Her hands rose to her face as if trying to blot out the fears filling her mind.

Lord, I can only imagine how scared she is. How do I help her? How do I stop the person after her and keep this from happening again?

"Flat tires are easy to fix and I'm sure getting the power back won't be that hard," he added, quickly. "I can call a mechanic and electrician for you."

"But they probably won't get here until morning." She paused a long moment, then laughed as if trying to cheer herself up. She looked at him. "Well, I told my great-aunt I didn't need a hotel room for tonight, but I guess now I do. Would you be able to give me a ride?"

"You can stay at our house with us," Kyle said. "Mom wouldn't hear of you going to a hotel."

"Thank you," Ophelia said.

Then suddenly, there was a faraway glimmer in her eyes

as if she'd just noticed something. He'd seen the same look on her face when she'd spotted the cuff link, back in the barn. But before he could ask her what she was thinking, she popped the trunk of her car and pulled out a gym bag. Then she went back to the house, grabbed her phone and purse off a table just inside the door, and joined him again.

They started walking, down the sidewalk and away from her house. Rocky walked a few steps ahead of them, glancing back every now and then as if double-checking he was on the right path. They took the long way back, along the twisting sidewalks instead of cutting through the backyards and parks that Kyle had taken to get there.

"There was an odd look on your face when I told you that my mom wouldn't hear of you going to a hotel," he said. "Like it had just sparked something in your mind. What was that about?"

"You noticed that?" she asked.

"Yeah, I did."

"I don't know if it's relevant," Ophelia said, after a long moment. "But what I suddenly remembered in the moment is that the masked man seemed almost surprised to see me there, as if he hadn't expected me to be home. Which I might not have been, because Gabrielle offered me Chloe's hotel room."

"The bridesmaid who didn't show," Kyle said.

"Yeah, and Aunt Evelyn really wanted me to stay with them all in the hotel. I called her before I went to bed. She was safe and told me that the hotel manager had reassured her they had security."

"So, you think she sent a masked man over to scare you into going there." The flippant words slipped his lips before he could catch himself. "Oh, I'm so sorry! That was a horrible joke!"

Ophelia laughed and punched him in the arm. "No, it's fine. I have to laugh or I'll cry."

He tapped her shoulder back, gently and softly, though, almost as if his knuckles were kissing her skin. "Well, if you need to cry, that's good with me, too. Everybody cries sometimes and I'm always down for a hug if you need it."

"Thank you," she said again. But this time, her voice barely rose above a whisper. She swallowed hard. They walked on. "Anyway, maybe our masked attacker thought I'd be at the hotel and that my house would be empty. Which could mean he's somehow connected to the wedding party, well enough to know who I am and where I live. He might even know I'm a backup bridesmaid."

"Now, that's a scary thought," he said. "What do you think he could have possibly wanted at your house?"

"I don't know," she admitted.

"Well, you can stay with us as long as you need," Kyle said. "We've got plenty of room. It used to be Kevin's house and they were planning for a large family. Most nights, the master bedroom is completely empty. I tend to sleep in Brody's room to help settle him if he wakes up in the night. Besides, my mother would never forgive me if I didn't insist."

She smiled. "Well, your mother did save my life, as did you."

He placed a quick call to his mom, who as expected was more than happy to have Ophelia stay with them. She'd said she'd make sure there were fresh towels, toiletries for her in the master bedroom's en suite, as well as getting one of the women from the church to drop off a bag of clothes from the donation room, even though he reassured her that Ophelia was bringing a bag. He thanked her and ended the call.

He filled Ophelia in on the conversation. Then they lapsed back into silence. Their footsteps were slow and easy, but still his mind raced with questions about the murder. If the case was connected to the Rocky Mountain Killer, then why had the white van followed them? Why had the masked man broken into Ophelia's house? Had there been something in her house he'd wanted to destroy? Surely he had to know that a crime scene investigator wouldn't take evidence home with her? And none of that matched any of the RMK's previous murders. And yet, why were there elements so similar to the RMK murders? Were they dealing with a copycat killer?

"Don't worry, we'll get answers tomorrow," Ophelia said softly, as if she'd been able to hear his thoughts.

"How did you know I was worrying about the case?" he asked.

"Your forehead was all scrunchy," she admitted. "But honestly, I was partly talking to myself."

He chuckled and they kept walking.

"Our main problem is that John Doe was killed after five and the lab doesn't run twenty-four hours a day," Ophelia said. "But it will open at nine tomorrow and we'll start processing samples then. Just know that it takes time. As I'm sure you've noticed, things in real-life labs go a lot slower than the ones on TV. But I promise I will do everything in my power to process the evidence quickly as possible. For now, all we can really do is guess what we'll find and talk ourselves around in circles."

Now, wasn't that true?

"You said you were getting a PhD?" he asked.

"Yes, in biology," she said. "My thesis has to do with using advances in DNA analysis to improve our understanding of the migratory practices of endangered species. As you know there's a lot of concern about the endangered wolf population in the Rocky Mountains, and my hope is to use recent advances in our understanding of mitochondrial DNA to find less intrusive ways of tracking their migratory routes. My hope is that scientists in other areas can then apply that research in their own work with endangered animals, to better understand their family lineage, migration habits and how to protect them."

"That's fascinating," he said.

As they passed under a golden lamplight, he watched as a smile lit up her face. It was stunning.

"I think so, too." She seemed genuinely delighted he'd asked.

"How are you getting a PhD while working full-time for the crime lab?" he asked. "Why not finish your PhD first?"

"Because I couldn't afford to," she said. Although they'd moved back into darkness, he could still hear the smile in her voice. "PhDs are expensive and I always wanted to work with the crime lab. I did get an amazing scholarship that covers some of the cost, but it doesn't cover basic living expenses and it requires me to hit some pretty rigorous deadlines. As hard as it is to do both at the same time, it would be even harder to give up on one of my dreams. Even if it doesn't leave any time for anything else."

"Yeah, I get that," he said. "I'm juggling my work with the MCK9 Task Force, the FBI and taking care of Brody." He felt a rueful smile cross his lips. "I love that little guy with my entire heart and would do anything for him. I just hope when he looks back on his life, he'll always know I loved him and not feel like he missed out on anything because his father was off chasing serial killers."

Rocky stopped walking suddenly and sat. Kyle looked around to realize their long, meandering walk had finally led back to his front door. He couldn't remember the last time he'd gone for a quiet nighttime stroll with anyone, let alone anyone whose company he enjoyed quite that much. And there was a good reason for that.

"If I'm honest," he said, "I know I keep saying I don't have time for a life outside of work and Brody, but it's deeper than that. I don't want drama that's going to impact my life and his. I don't want to go through all the ups and downs of even trying to date anyone. Remember how I told you a few hours ago that my brother was the brave one and I always admired that about him?"

"I do." Ophelia nodded.

"Well, I think the bravest thing he ever did was choosing to get married and have a family. My dad was really terrible. He drank and yelled and treated my mother like trash. Finally, she left him when Kevin and I were still in elementary school. But he'd still show up drunk and try to start fights, or he'd call from jail when he needed someone to bail him out, until finally he ended his own life when I was twenty-two."

He hadn't even realized that he'd crossed his arms tightly across his chest, until he felt Ophelia reach for his hand. Gently she brushed her fingers along his and there was something about the simple gesture that said more than a thousand words ever could.

"I'm not afraid I'll ever turn into a man like my father." Slowly he unfolded his arms, took her hand and squeezed it for a long moment, before letting it go. "What scares me is knowing an incredible woman like my mother somehow fell in love with someone who made us so miserable. I never want to put Brody through anything like that. Not even the whole uncertainty of dating and breakups. He deserves certainty and stability, and I need to give him that."

"Yeah, I get that," Ophelia said.

"Well, thanks for listening," he said. "I don't tend to open up to people but you're really easy to talk to."

"You are, too."

They walked up the driveway and into the house, where Rocky promptly wandered off down the hall in the direction of Brody's room, probably to look for Taffy. Kyle had expected his mom to be waiting up for them in the open-concept living room/dining room. But it was empty except for a handwritten note from Alice to Ophelia welcoming her to their home and telling her where to find anything she might need. She'd also left a tray of hot lavender tea and homemade pound cake for Ophelia in her room.

She thanked him again, and he knew he should say good-night, but instead he stood there, with her blue-eyed gaze looking up into his face as he awkwardly went over all the same things, from mugs to towels, that he was sure his mom had mentioned in her note.

"The master bedroom is on the opposite side of the house than the other two bedrooms," he said and pointed, "and has its own bathroom. There should be a charger by the bed you can use for your phone. Mom's room and Brody's room are down that way. We tend to get up really early and I have a team meeting via video chat at eight. I'd really like you to be there and a part of it. Not just because you have a connection to Jared and there's a good possibility you'll be able to get vital information about this murder we won't be able to get any other way, but also because I really appreciate your professional insight."

"You don't know how much it's meant to me to spend some time talking with someone who really understands my work," she said. "Evelyn and Jared don't get it. They think it's weird at best and gross at worst, and I feel sometimes like they're embarrassed of me."

"Are you kidding?" Kyle said. "Ophelia, in case I haven't made myself clear by now, I think you are an absolutely incredible crime scene investigator. I'm overjoyed every time I know you're processing one of my crime scenes because it means that nothing is going to get missed and everything is going to go smoothly. Because you're good. You're like really, really good at your job. You should feel proud. Don't ever let anyone take that from you."

Her lips parted as if his rambling words had suddenly robbed her of her breath. For a long moment she didn't say anything. Then she dropped her bag, threw her arms around his neck and hugged him tightly.

"Thanks," she said. "I really needed that."

"Well, it's true."

He wrapped his arms around her and held her to his chest, blindsided by just how perfect and wonderful it felt to have her in his arms. Then slowly they both pulled away, their fingertips brushing as they stepped apart.

"Good night, Agent West," she said. "I think you're pretty incredible at your job, too."

"Thank you." He smiled. "Good night, CSI Clarke."

Then she picked up her bag, turned and walked down the hallway, leaving him standing there wondering why his heart was racing.

She expected to toss and turn the way she normally did, as her busy mind struggled to slow down and rest. After all, a criminal had broken into her home. But maybe Alice's kind snack of pound cake and tea had settled her stomach. Or there was just something safe and comforting about being in Kyle's home. So as she lay there in the darkness and prayed, still in the same gray tracksuit, she found a peace that surpassed her own understanding sweeping through her heart, and Ophelia fell into a deep and peaceful sleep.

She woke hours later to the sound of tiny feet pattering up and down the hallway outside her door, along with a chorus of jingling dog tags and a child's laughter. Ophelia sat up slowly and stretched, thanking God for her good night's sleep and the safe haven she'd found. Sun streamed through a large window that looked out on a toy-strewn backyard. The bed itself had simple wooden frame and a beautiful handmade quilt that had somehow been cozy without being too hot for a June Santa Fe night. The sounds of footsteps and giggling stopped suddenly with a muffled thud that seemed to hit the door.

She swung her legs over the edge of the bed and stood.

"Is everyone, okay?" she called.

"We okay!" a small voice chirped from the other side of the door.

She smiled. "You sure?"

"Yeah!" More giggles.

She crossed the floor and opened the door to see a small barefoot boy in firefighter pajamas and the puppy who looked like a miniature of Rocky sprawled on the floor.

"Why, hello," she said.

The boy and dog untangled themselves. Taffy licked her fingers. The small dog's tail wagged rapid-fire from one side to the other. Brody looked at Ophelia skeptically.

She crouched down until she was eye level with the toddler.

"You must be Brody," she said softly. "I'm your daddy's work friend. My name is Ophelia."

"O'Felly," Brody repeated, confidently. He frowned. "You not sleeping."

She assumed someone had told him that she was and so had instructed him to be quiet.

"No, I'm not sleeping now," she agreed. "But I was sleeping before. So thank you for being so good and quiet."

"Yes!" He nodded as if agreeing with her assessment. A huge smile spread across the small boy's face.

Seemed she'd hit upon the right answer. "It's nice to meet you."

She stretched out her hand to shake his. He slapped it hard in an enthusiastic and cheerful high five, and then took off running back down the hall again with Taffy at his heels.

She stood up slowly and watched them scamper, feeling something warm and soft glow inside her chest. So, that was Brody. He was absolutely adorable. Just as the little boy reached the living room, turned around and was about to run back toward her, Kyle appeared from somewhere out of view, scooped Brody into his arms and lifted up him.

"I good!" Brody told him, loudly.

"You often are," Kyle said, with a chuckle.

Then he glanced from the squirming toddler in his arms, down the hall to where Ophelia still stood in the doorway.

"Good morning," he called. "How did you sleep?"

"A lot better than I was expecting." She ran her fingers through her long and tangled hair.

"I hope we didn't wake you," Kyle said.

"No, not at all," she said.

"I'm glad." He shifted Kyle around onto his hip. "I'm about to feed the kid and dogs, then make some scrambled eggs and toast for myself, if that's okay by you. I've already put the coffee on. It should be ready in a moment."

"Sounds wonderful," she said.

Brody wriggled in Kyle's grasp.

"Daddy! Down!" he ordered. Kyle broke her gaze and set Brody on the floor. "Want outside!"

"Later," he said. "You can play outside after breakfast and Daddy's video call."

She closed the door, leaned against it and pressed her hand to her chest. She could feel her heartbeat racing against her palm as if she'd just run a marathon. Whatever this was that she was feeling right now, she had to nip it in the bud and fast. It was one thing to fall into a strong man's supportive arms in a moment of crisis. It was another thing to let herself stay there—especially when the last thing he wanted was a relationship and the last thing she needed was to let herself be distracted from her work. The opportunity she'd been given through getting a funding grant for her PhD was a once-in-a-lifetime thing. She'd never have been able to afford it without help, and if she lost this grant she couldn't imagine ever landing another one.

She might not have wanted to be a bridesmaid but had even less desire to be seen as a damsel in distress who relied on someone like Kyle to save her and risked blowing her PhD grant and life goals over some foolish romantic attraction. She shuddered to think how Kyle—a man who'd told her repeatedly that he wasn't looking for a relationship—would react if he knew she had a bit of a crush on him. He'd be uncomfortable. Maybe even horrified. Especially if he thought she was at risk of putting her crush on him above her career and studies. Either way, it wouldn't exactly help her career if one of the top FBI agents in New Mexico decided he didn't want her working on his cases.

She could still hear Kyle's cheerful voice coming from

the large living room and kitchen area as he called to the dogs that breakfast was ready, and the clatter of paws and dog tags as Rocky and Taffy ran to their bowls. Brody's voice babbled in a cheerful mixture of real words and nonsense.

Her phone was fully charged from having been plugged in the night before. She already had a message from her boss at the crime lab, telling her that he'd heard about the shooting at the ranch and not to worry about coming in for work if she needed to take the day off. Not that she was planning on taking him up on that. Then there was the fact that Jared and Gabrielle were still supposed to get married that night.

Lord, please help me just focus on the tasks at hand and get through them.

Framed pictures hung on the wall across from the bed of a happy couple on their wedding day, who she assumed were Brody's parents, both by themselves and with a beaming Kyle and Alice. Another showed Kevin and Kyle with their arms around each other as teenagers and still another showed Kyle's sister-in-law with baby Brody in her arms.

A sudden wash of pain swept over Ophelia's heart as she remembered the stories Kyle had told her the night before. Alice had been hurt by her husband. Kyle and Kevin had lost their father. Then Brody had lost his parents.

Lord, they've seen so much loss and yet they've never let their hearts grow angry and bitter. Bless them, dear God. Help me to be a blessing to them. Please help us all solve these terrible murders before somebody else gets hurts. Help me to honor You and do my utmost whatever this case throws at me next. And please, keep my heart and mind from all distractions.

Including a handsome face with dark and fathomless eyes.

It was almost fifteen minutes later when she'd finished getting changed into the slacks and top she kept in her gym bag, packed up her stuff and walked back out into the living room and kitchen area. Her lab didn't open until nine, and even then, she wasn't expected in. She placed a quick call to her boss, got his voice mail, and left a message saying there'd been a break-in at her house the night before and she didn't have access to her laptop but that all of her research was saved on a secure cloud server. She then called the electric company who said they'd have someone out right away to check on the power at her house, and her regular mechanic who said he'd get one of his guys to pop over and replace her tires. Both assured her she didn't have to be there and they'd take care of it. She felt relieved.

Then, finally she walked into the main room to find Kyle sitting at the head of the kitchen table facing the back deck, with his laptop open in front of him and Rocky sitting by his feet. To his left, Brody sat in his high chair pushing around serial squares and banana pieces on the tray, occasionally dropping one over the edge for roly-poly Taffy to scramble after. The chair to his right was empty but set with a beautiful yellow place mat, cutlery and a glass of orange juice.

He stood as she walked into the room. So did Rocky.

"There you are," Kyle said with a grin and for a long moment his eyes seemed to linger on her face. "There are eggs in the griddle and coffee in the pot. There's bread in the toaster, too, but I didn't pop it down so that it wouldn't be cold by the time you were ready for it." He ran both hands along the side of his jeans. "I'm sorry it's not much, but we weren't expecting company."

"Don't worry, it's absolutely wonderful," Ophelia said.

"I can't remember the last time I had a home-cooked meal. Most nights I just put something from the grocery-store freezer section into the microwave. Then I fall asleep reading and end up grabbing a yogurt and cup of coffee on the way out the door."

Another reason why dating was out of the question. What man wanted to come over on a Friday night to pull back the plastic wrap on a frozen entrée?

"Well, I never mind cooking," Kyle said. "It's the one thing that relaxes me. Mom and I have worked out a pretty good pattern here of divvying up the chores inside the house. It's the yard work that gets to me, because Mom can't do it while watching Brody and by the time I get home it's dark."

"That's the one thing I am good at," Ophelia said. "Because I listen to research and audio books for my PhD for hours on the weekend while I weed and mow."

"Maybe we should start trading yard work for leftovers," Kyle said, with a chuckle. He ran his hand over the back of his neck. "Anyway, I set a place for you to come join us at the table when you're ready."

She walked into the kitchen area, poured herself a cup of coffee, added a dash of cream and inhaled the aroma deeply.

"I've already got through to the power company and my mechanic," she said. "They both assure me they'll be out soon."

"Good," Kyle said. "I was going to call them myself and then figured it was better I check with you first. My mom's running errands now. Knowing her, she'll come back with enough food to feed an army."

Then he frowned slightly.

"Everything okay?" she asked.

"Yeah, I hope so," he said. "My mom's been going to the

pharmacy a lot recently. Specifically, one on the other side of town. She assures me there's nothing to worry about and the pharmacist there is just really good at recommending vitamins and supplements for her joint stiffness, but I worry."

"I get that," Ophelia said. "Truth is, I'm really worried about my great-aunt Evelyn. Before everything kicked off yesterday with the murder of John Doe, I had the odd sense that something was wrong and she was worried. But she wouldn't talk about it."

She scooped some scrambled eggs onto a plate she found waiting for her on the counter, then popped a bite into her mouth. Sprinkled with some kind of spice and cheese, the eggs were delicious. She topped up her coffee and then carried her plate around to the empty place waiting for her at the table. She sat.

"Evelyn was a model when she was younger," she said, "and did a lot of regional pageants and briefly ran charm classes for young women. She really values putting on a good face and isn't the kind of person who complains or would open up about something that's bothering her. But if she did know something—anything at all—that she thought could be related to the murder in the barn, I know she wouldn't hesitate to tell the police." She sighed. "As you know, I called her last night before the intruder broke in. And I don't want to tell her about that, because she will be beside herself with worry. I don't want to upset her that badly. Or steal the thunder from Jared's wedding day, if he's still getting married today."

"I hope for their sake the death of John Doe had nothing to do with their wedding," he said. "Although sadly we can't rule that out. But I did have a quick chat with Patricia this morning and she told me everyone was fine overnight at the hotel and that she'd email me an update on their end of the case soon. I've got to jump in a video call meeting with my team in a few minutes. I've already briefed Chase quickly over the phone, so they should be up to speed more or less, on what happened that night. After we wrap up, we'll see about heading back to your house. I don't think you should go back there alone."

"Thank you." The desire to be independent and sort her own problems didn't change the fact that she also didn't want to just blindly walk into danger. Thankfully, Kyle didn't seem like the kind of guy who'd judge her over something like that.

The adults finished their breakfast, then Ophelia cleared the dishes while Kyle pulled Brody from his high chair, helped him wash his hands and then set him up with a box full of toys on the living room carpet.

"Want outside!" Brody said.

Ophelia glanced out the glass doors. The modest backyard was completely fenced in and included a sandbox, swing set and a myriad of toddler toys.

"I know, buddy," Kyle said. "But I just need to talk to work on my computer first. I'll take you outside when I'm done. But now I need you to be quiet." Kyle ran his finger across his lips in an invisible zipper. "Why don't you make Taffy an imaginary cake?"

Brody's lower lip stuck out, but he sat politely on the carpet and began pulling plastic pots and pans out of a bin. Taffy scampered over and flopped on the floor against him.

Kyle pulled the chair that Ophelia had been sitting on next to his and started the call. "Sorry we're going to have to share the screen."

"No problem." She held up the coffeepot. "Do you want a refill?"

"Yes, please," he said. "Just black."

She carried the pot over, topped up his mug and then sat down beside him. They were sitting so close she could feel his knee brush against hers.

She watched as three video call boxes opened one by one on the screen.

A man she assumed was Chase Rawlston was first. The task force leader had a strong jaw, broad shoulders and a cheerful-looking golden retriever poking his head into the frame. Chase welcomed them to the call and introduced his dog as Dash, before instructing him to go lie down. Next came US Marshal Meadow Ames, an athletic woman with long brown hair and bright green eyes. Her beautiful tan vizsla, Grace, lay on a bed behind her. The final face to pop up was Isla. The technical analyst had one of the most beautiful smiles Ophelia had ever seen, despite the sadness that lurked in her dark-eyed gaze.

Lord, whatever the struggles are that Isla's going through, please be with her and help her.

"It's nice to meet you, Ophelia," Chase said. "Thank you for joining us. How are you feeling this morning? I was so sorry to hear about what happened last night."

"I'm good," Ophelia said. "Thankfully, Kyle and Rocky were there when I needed them."

"Chase briefed us on what happened," Meadow said. "The whole situation sounds genuinely terrifying. And I'm really glad you're okay and I'm impressed at how you handled the whole thing."

"And I'm impressed by the fact that he said you bit the

guy!" Isla said. "It's just too bad you didn't get any DNA or we could've tested it."

She laughed. Ophelia did, too. She could see why Kyle liked his team.

"Ophelia was brilliant," Kyle said and she felt her cheeks glow under his praise. "I've also been working closely with Detective Patricia Gonzales of the Santa Fe PD and she'll be emailing me any moment with an update on what they've found from their end."

"I'm going to be sending Meadow and her partner, Grace, out your way as well when we wrap up the call," Chase said. "It's clear that whoever you're after won't hesitate to strike where you live, and, Kyle, I think it's important that Alice and Brody have some protection."

Ophelia watched as Kyle swallowed hard.

"Thank you," he said.

"I think we need to discuss moving your mom and Brody into a safe house," Meadow said. "But we can talk about that when I get there."

Kyle glanced to where Brody and the puppy now sat playing happily on the carpet, and she could almost see him weighing being away from the little boy against the desire not to put him in danger. "Okay."

"Do you have any new evidence for us in terms of identifying who this John Doe was?" Chase asked. "Or linking it to the Rocky Mountain Killer?"

"Not yet," Ophelia said. "The lab was already closed for the day when the scene was processed, and I'm afraid we don't have a night crew. But they open at nine, and will be working on it this morning."

"I'm looking forward to finding out John Doe's identity," Kyle said, "and if he has any connection to the Young Rancher's Club."

"We all re," Chase said. "His photo didn't match anything in our system or anyone we know who was related to Elk Valley."

"The bride from the wedding, Gabrielle, also had a stalker who we only know as Bobby," Ophelia said. "It's possible that either he's John Doe, or that he's our shooter."

"Well, hopefully, a DNA match will tell us who this guy is," Chase said. "Isla, if you could coordinate with Ophelia directly on any evidence as it comes in that would be great."

"Absolutely," Isla said. "I'm especially interested in that cuff link and also seeing if the bullets found at this crime scene were all fired from the same 9mm gun as the other six murders. It'll give me a break from trying to track down rhinestone dog collars."

Ophelia remembered what Kyle had told her the night before about how the serial killer had kidnapped Cowgirl, a compassion therapy labradoodle that belonged to the task force. Then recently the killer had sent Chase a picture of Cowgirl from a burner phone that showed the dog wearing a pink collar that read Killer.

"Any success on that?" Kyle asked.

"Not yet," Isla said. "It's a popular collar, sold in at least fifty shops across the Rocky Mountain region."

"I did get another taunting text about Cowgirl from the RMK," Chase said, grimly, "telling me he thinks the dog could be pregnant."

"Whoa." Kyle sucked in a breath and Ophelia's heart ached. The pain in his face was echoed in those of his team. She knew how much Kyle loved Rocky. She couldn't imagine how the unit felt in losing one of their K-9 dogs, only to have her kidnapped and now potentially be pregnant.

Kyle's phone pinged and Ophelia watched as he reached for it.

"I've got an update from Patricia," he said, his eyes scanning the screen. "The white van was stolen from a Santa Fe laundry delivery service yesterday and found on the outskirts of town in the early hours of the morning. Apparently, he torched it before abandoning it."

"To destroy evidence," Ophelia and Isla said in unison. Then they both laughed.

"Nobody's found the silver car the killer used to drive away from the murder scene," Kyle went on. "But judging by the state the van was found in, they're guessing that wherever it is, he trashed it, too. Also, according to Patricia, a gas station attendant recognized our John Doe, and while the guy didn't get a license plate, he did say that John Doe was driving a silver car that matches the description of the one our masked man drove off in. Police are guessing John Doe parked his car out of sight and walked the rest of the way to Cherish Ranch, and then the killer stole his car for an easy getaway. Apparently our victim had stopped at the gas station to ask for directions to Cherish Ranch—specifically the barn. The gas station attendant said he had plans to meet someone special there."

"So he was lured to his death," Chase said. "Just like the RMK's other victims. The question is, was John Doe killed by the RMK? Or are we dealing with a copycat?"

SIX

"Let's hash this out," Chase said, "go over the evidence and see where we end up. Kyle, you argue for this being the RMK and I'll present the evidence against."

"Well, the victim is a young man," Kyle said, "who was shot once in the chest at close range, after being lured to a barn, in Rocky Mountain country. That all lines up."

"But we have no known link to the Young Rancher's Club or Elk Valley," Chase countered. "Also, he doesn't match the age profile of the other victims. The first three victims were in their late teens and early twenties. The other three were killed ten years later, but would've been the same age as the first three at the time of the first three murders. John Doe would've been nine or ten at that time. Way too young to be a member of YRC or friends with any of the members."

"Also, I'm guessing the other murders happened at isolated locations," Ophelia said, "not one in the middle of a wedding weekend."

"Hey, whose side are you on?" Kyle joked. "But you're right, this took place at a very public wedding event. There must be dozens, if not hundreds, of other barns in the area the RMK could've chosen."

"Which might be an escalation," Meadow said, "or a coincidence."

"Or it means it's not linked at all," Chase said.

"Outside now!" Brody called. The little boy climbed to his feet and toddled toward the door.

"I'm happy to take him outside," Ophelia told Kyle, "if that's okay with you." She had a feeling that her part of the call was wrapping up anyway, and it would also give Kyle the freedom to talk more freely if he wanted to discuss any of the more gruesome details of the crime without risking Brody's little ears overhearing anything.

Kyle searched her face. "You sure?"

"Absolutely," she said. "Would it be okay with you if I checked my phone and made a couple of quick calls while I'm out?"

"Yeah," he said. "The backyard is completely fenced in and I can also keep an eye on him through the window. I just don't want him out there alone. Thanks."

She said a quick goodbye to the team, telling Meadow that she'd see her in person soon and Isla that she'd see her online. Then she thanked them all again, went to put her shoes on and headed to where Brody now stood looking out the back door.

"You outside?" Brody asked, hopefully.

"Yes," she said. "Let's go outside while your daddy finishes his call. Can you show me your backyard?"

"Yes!" His little hand reached up, grabbed her fingers and squeezed them. Something fluttered in her chest.

She opened the door. Brody dropped her hand and ran out into the yard at full speed with Taffy at his heels. Boy and dog tumbled into the grass together. She glanced back at Kyle. Something unspoken moved through his gaze.

"All good, Kyle?" she asked.

"Yeah." His Adam's apple bobbed. "See you in a bit."

She closed the sliding door and turned back to the yard, where Brody and Taffy were now playing tug-of-war with a soft plastic disk. Then she sat down on a bench and checked her messages. Her boss had texted to thank her for the call and to say that he'd have a backup laptop available at her workstation when she got in.

That made two things she could thank God for.

But worryingly, she'd missed three calls from Evelyn.

Fear rattled her heart. Quickly, she dialed her back. Her great-aunt answered on the fourth ring. "Aunt Evelyn! Hi! Is everything all right! Is everyone okay?"

"Of course, dear," Evelyn said. "Don't be all dramatic. I just wanted to let you know to be at the hotel at four thirty for hair and makeup. The photographer's booked for six."

"Right, for the wedding." Her mind flashed to where she'd left the bridesmaid's dress crumpled in her clothes hamper. Between John Doe's blood and the smoke from the fire, she couldn't imagine how bad it must look, and smell. "That's still happening today?"

"Please don't start on with me about that," Evelyn said. "We have enough chaos going on over here with Jared and Gabrielle trying to find an alternative spot at the ranch to hold their wedding reception tonight, and her parents' flight being delayed again. Poor Gabrielle has been in floods of tears all morning. She and Jared are on their way to Cherish Ranch right now to see what can be salvaged of their original plans. I know the bride and groom aren't traditionally supposed to see each other before the wedding, but Jared didn't want Gabrielle having to deal with everything on her own. My Jared is a very good boy—"

Ophelia bit her lip and stopped from pointing out he was thirty-one, the same as she was.

"And he's been really good to Gabrielle," her great-aunt went on. "You know I'm pretty choosy about who I think is good enough for you two. But she's perfect. Beautiful, wealthy, well connected. I couldn't have found a better match for him myself. But Jared is so frustrated with the ranch for trying to cancel or scale back the wedding. The police won't let them use the barn and the ranch is suggesting a quiet ceremony at the outdoor, cliffside chapel, with a downsized reception. But Gabrielle and Jared have already paid for the dinner and still want the day to feel special. Really, all he and Gabrielle want to do is put the whole unfortunate situation behind them."

Ophelia felt her fingers clench. Didn't Jared realize how self-centered he was being?

"It's not like they had a kitchen flood or something," Ophelia said. "It was a murder, Auntie. A man was shot yesterday."

And the killer was still on the loose.

"I know what happened and how terrible it was," Evelyn chided. "But this is your cousin's special day, it's his decision and we need to focus on being happy for him and Gabrielle. I'm sure Gabrielle and Jared would appreciate if you dropped by the ranch to help them, before you came to the hotel. Also, she said to remind you to check out the social media page they made about the wedding. They'll be posting all their updates there."

Ophelia had vaguely known there was one, but hadn't even looked at it yet.

"Whee!" Brody shouted cheerfully as he dashed across

the yard, holding the plastic disk out in front of him like a steering wheel. "I go! Fast!"

Taffy barked cheerfully, chasing after Brody, and pretended to nip at his heels.

"What's that?" Evelyn said. "Where are you?"

"That's Brody," Ophelia said. "He's the son of my agent friend Kyle West, who questioned everyone yesterday. There was a trespasser at my house last night, but he ran off and I'm fine," she added quickly as she heard Evelyn gasp. "You don't need to worry. But Kyle and his mother said I could stay with them."

"And you're dating the handsome policeman from my phone app?"

Well, she didn't have to sound so shocked.

"We're friends," Ophelia said. "And he's an FBI agent. As I told you, I knew him from work."

"Well, you tell your friend Kyle that he's very welcome to come to the wedding as your date," Evelyn said. "I'll fire off a quick message to Jared and Gabrielle letting them know."

"You really don't need to do that…"

"Pfft, Gabrielle was already worried you didn't have a plus-one and I'm sure she'll be happy to know you that you're bringing your gentleman friend."

Gentleman friend.

She glanced over her shoulder to where Kyle sat at the table talking to his team on video chat. His dark eyes flickered to her face and then looked back down at the screen.

Well, Kyle was definitely a gentleman in all the best meanings of the word.

And yes, she would feel really blessed to have him as a friend.

"I'm sure everyone would be happy to see him," Evelyn added.

Ophelia wasn't as sure about that as her aunt was, especially if anyone there had something to hide. But she also knew that Kyle might appreciate the opportunity to attend the wedding, talk to people and see if he could discover anything new about the case.

She ended the call with her aunt, telling her that she loved her and reminding her to stay safe. Then she prayed.

Lord, this wedding is the last thing on my mind right now. I'm frustrated by the fact that part of me suspects that my cousin is a self-centered man who doesn't even realize how hard it would be for ranch staff to work today or that some guests might not want to go back on that property after what happened. People need time to heal. Please, help me let go of my judgment and anger. Help me be there for my family and do my job.

After all, she loved her cousin, and if she missed his wedding she'd regret it for the rest of her life.

"Look!" Brody ran toward her and held out his hand. She looked into his grubby little hands. It was a rock. "See!"

"Oh, nice!" His enthusiasm and joy tugged at her heartstrings.

"Yes!" Brody turned and ran to the sandbox, where he started noisily pushing the rock around with a plastic truck.

Ophelia opened the wedding's page on the social media site. She'd avoided it for months, but it probably was good she'd checked it before the wedding. The top post was a new picture of Gabrielle and Jared holding hands, along with an emotional message about how deeply they loved each other, how sad they were for the tragedy that happened and how determined they were not to let it get in the way of starting their life together.

A flashing blue circle at the bottom of the screen told Ophelia that someone had tried to send her a message via the social media site, which was odd, as everyone she knew who'd be at the wedding had her cell phone number.

She clicked on the message. Text on the screen told her that she'd received a video message from Chloe Madison.

Gabrielle's roommate? The bridesmaid who hadn't shown up, whom Ophelia had been asked to replace? The time stamp showed the message had been sent at two thirty in the afternoon, yesterday. Hours before Gabrielle had asked Ophelia to be in the wedding party. She clicked on the message. Up came the face of a young woman, who looked to be in her early twenties, with long red hair and a gold, heart-shaped locket around her neck.

"Hi." Chloe's face filled the screen. She had the look of someone who was upset but trying very hard to be calm in order to be taken seriously. "We've never met. But I know you're Jared's cousin and I'm Gabrielle's roommate. Umm. We need to talk before the wedding. It's really important. I'm coming to Santa Fe early and maybe we can meet up. Message me here and don't tell anybody I contacted you. But I think something bad is going to go down with Gabrielle's ex-boyfriend Bobby."

After the team call officially ended, Chase and Meadow logged off, and Kyle stayed on for a few moments to talk to Isla. He'd felt a special kind of compassion for Isla, ever since discovering the single technical analyst had given up on love and decided to adopt, knowing that she'd chosen the same challenging and rewarding path that he was on. They'd bonded over his journey of becoming a sudden parent to Brody, and Kyle had thanked God when Isla was certified as a foster mother and had received her first photos of a newborn baby girl named Charisse.

But then, Isla's dreams had been dashed when the private Christian Foster-Adoption Agency had denied her application after someone had called anonymously and reported her as unfit. The injustice of the accusation and the fact that it could be made about someone as wonderful as Isla still burned in the back of Kyle's throat.

"A few weeks ago," Kyle said, "I asked you to make a list of anyone you could think of who might have ever felt slighted by you and decided to sabotage your attempt to become a mother." He'd asked her while they'd both been investigating with the task force in Sagebrush, Idaho, and staying at Deputy Selena Smith's place. Isla had left Wyoming for a few days to help the task force but also to get some R and R after her application had been denied. "Have you given any more thought to that?"

"Yes." Isla frowned. "But it's a pretty short list and nothing has really clicked yet. There are three different men who I dated briefly but decided not to see again. None of those relationships raised any red flags, but some people are able to hide their true nature. Also, I had a falling-out with a cousin last Thanksgiving, over her plan to bring her boyfriend to family dinner. He was a petty criminal and I thought she was in denial over just how scummy this guy was. They're still dating. He's in jail now, so he's not the one who placed the call. I don't want to think that my cousin could've done that to me." Isla's shoulders rose and fell. "But I'll go see if I can visit her and talk to her. I'll look into those three former dates, too."

Kyle told her that he'd pray for her and to contact him at any time if there was anything he could do to help. As Kyle ended the call, he sat for a long moment, and looked out the back window, to where Ophelia was crouched down beside Brody in the sandbox, playing trucks with him, much to the toddler's delight. It seemed Ophelia and Brody were deep in conversation. He couldn't hear what they were saying, but whatever it was had Ophelia tossing her head back in fits of laughter while Brody giggled. Something warmed in his chest, as if the simple interaction had lit the tiny pilot light of a fire that had gone out long ago. If it had ever burned at all.

How ironic that his mom had resorted to creating an online dating profile for him to try to find him a wife, when this incredibly beautiful and kindhearted woman had been under his nose all along, working alongside him, excelling at a job that meant everything to people like him and helping him do the work that mattered most.

Only, she wasn't exactly applying for the job of wife to an FBI agent, K-9 task force member and mother to his toddler.

Nor was he ever going to ask her to.

Lord, I keep telling You that I'm not looking to start a romance with anyone. And I'm really not. I don't have the time to give a woman the attention and care she deserves from a man courting her. I feel like I'm barely giving Brody the attention he deserves, and the last thing I want to do is bring uncertainty, conflict or tension into Brody's life. Please help clear my heart and my mind from whatever nonsense that's clouding it now, so I can focus on solving this case, before anybody else gets hurt.

He stood up and walked over to the sliding glass door

that led to the outside. Rocky rose from his usual post on the floor by his feet and followed. But as he reached the door, Ophelia looked up, as if sensing his gaze. Their eyes met across his son's head, through the yard and the glass of the sliding back door, and for a long moment neither of them looked away.

The door opened and closed behind him. He turned to see Alice walking in.

"Hey, Mom." He smiled. "Ophelia's outside with Brody. I'll introduce you in a moment."

"Sounds wonderful." Alice smiled back and set a bright green bag down on the counter.

"You've been to the pharmacy again," he said, frowning. "Is everything okay, Mom? That's the second trip to the pharmacy this week."

"I'm fine," Alice said. There was a smile on her face, but he noticed his mother wasn't meeting his eye. "I just picked up some sunscreen."

"Are you sure?" he said. "You set up a dating profile for me without telling me."

"I'm really sorry for that," she said. "I wasn't thinking. Please forgive me."

"Of course, Mom."

"Gramma!" Brody yipped, suddenly spotting her. He leaped to his feet and charged toward the door. Ophelia stood slowly and ran her hands down her pants. Sand and grass streaked her previously pristine clothes, but she didn't seem to mind. Kyle slid the door open and stepped back as Brody raced through, past him and into his grandmother's arms, as Alice crouched down and reached for him.

"Hey, Bo!" Alice scooped him into his arms. "Were you having fun in the sandbox?"

"Yes! Snack?" he asked, hopefully.

"You need to wash your hands first," Alice told her grandson as he pressed his hands against her cheeks leaving sand in their wake. She shifted Brody onto her hip, wiped her cheeks and then walked Brody over to the kitchen sink.

Rocky slipped out the door past Kyle, brushing against Kyle's legs in hello as he passed. Rocky and Taffy ran toward each other in a flurry of wagging tails and playful growls as they launched themselves into a pretend fight.

Ophelia dodged her way around the obstacle course of darting hounds and made her way to the door, which Kyle was still holding open for her. She slid in past him and their arms bumped. "Judging by all the comings and goings through that door, if you don't close it soon you'll be stuck holding it open all day."

"Yeah." He chuckled. "It feels like some days all I do is open and close the door so that two dogs and a kid can run in and out."

But he had to admit that although life had thrown him a pretty big curve ball, he really did enjoy sharing it with Rocky, Taffy and Brody.

"I saw you on the phone," Kyle said, keeping his voice low enough that Alice and Brody wouldn't catch it as they noisily washed their hands. "Is everything okay?"

"I don't know," she said. Her smile faded. "No specific emergencies and everyone seems to be safe. Jared and Gabrielle are at the ranch now trying to make new arrangements for their wedding and you've been invited to come now, as my plus-one. But I got a really worrying video message from Chloe, the missing bridesmaid, wanting to talk to me about Bobby. She seemed a bit scattered and I messaged her back, but she didn't reply."

"Got it," he said. "I'll just say a quick hi to Mom and then we'll head out in a second."

"I should really get changed first," she said. "Thankfully your mom laid out some clothes for me to borrow."

He turned to where Alice was standing at the kitchen sink with Brody, helping him wash his hands under the running water.

"Mom, this is Ophelia Clarke," he said. "Ophelia, this is my incredible mother, Alice West."

"It's so nice to meet you properly." Ophelia walked toward her. "I can't thank you enough for your help and for your hospitality last night. I don't know where I'd be if you hadn't answered that video call."

"Don't mention it," Alice said. "I'm just thankful for those moments when the Lord puts the right person in our life at the right time."

Kyle and his mom had never really talked about that turbulent time she'd gone through leaving her chaotic husband, taking her two young sons with her. It wasn't something she liked talking about. And most of the time he was just amazed that she still held out hope in the power of love. But she had told him that it had taken a lot of help and support, from friends, strangers at charities and the police. He knew that she was endlessly thankful to everyone who'd been there for her.

Both she and Kevin had found a way to make peace with their past. But still, when he looked at the precious child in Alice's arms, he couldn't imagine himself ever risking bringing a new prospective mother into Brody's life. What if Kyle failed to make the relationship work? And Brody ended up getting hurt by the fallout?

"Just promise me when the moment comes you'll pay the

kindness forward to somebody else who needs it," Alice added.

"I will," Ophelia said.

Alice turned off the water, set Brody down on the floor and grabbed a hand towel. Brody scampered away before his grandmother could try to dry his hands. She laughed, wiped her own hands across the towel and then reached for Ophelia.

The two woman clasped hands in greeting.

"It's just so nice to finally meet you," Alice said, as the two women pulled away again. "Kyle has been talking about you for months. It's been CSI Clarke this and CSI Clarke that. I lost count of the number of times my son told me that he was thankful to get to a crime scene and know that you were part of the team processing it, because he knew nothing would be missed."

"Really?" Ophelia asked. Her eyes widened and she turned to Kyle. He felt heat rise to the back of his neck.

"Professionally," Kyle said. "About your work, I had no idea who you were as a person." Or that she was beautiful, sweet and kind, with a smile that made his heart flutter. She'd been nothing to him but a figure in scrubs and a name on an evidence bag. "I just told her how much I appreciated your work as a CSI. Which, as you know, I do."

Her lips parted and then closed again. But not like she was embarrassed, more like she was too pleased by the compliment to figure out that to say.

"Speaking of which, Ophelia and I need to get to work," Kyle added. He kept his voice light, knowing Brody was still in earshot. "My colleague Meadow Ames and her K-9, Grace, are on their way here to provide us some additional backup, specifically to make sure you and Brody are safe.

They might stay here with us or take you, Brody and Taffy on a fun overnight vacation with them to a safe house."

Alice nodded and it was clear in her eyes that she took his meaning.

"Well, I'll make up a bed in the study for now if Meadow does stay," she said, "and start packing a bag if we do decide to take a trip."

He slipped one arm around her slender shoulders in a hug. "Thanks, Mom."

"Just give me a second," Ophelia said. "I've got to go wash this sand off me."

She slipped down the hall back into the master bedroom, and returned a few moments later in clean tan slacks, a tank top and a loose-fitting, short-sleeved, button-up white shirt that was tied at the waist.

Hang on, that was *his* shirt.

"Everything okay?" she asked, self-consciously. She slung her bag over one shoulder. "You're staring like I've got mud on my face."

"No," he said. "You look fine. That's just my dress shirt you're wearing."

"Oh." Her cheeks went pink. "I'm so sorry, I just found it in the room with the other clothes and assumed it was something Alice found. I can go find something else to wear if you want."

"No, it's okay. It actually looks really good on you."

Better than he liked to admit.

A few minutes later, Ophelia, Kyle and Rocky were climbing back in his SUV, ready to head to Ophelia's house.

"So, let's see that video message from Chloe," he said. She handed him the phone and he watched the video twice. When he was done, he whistled and leaned back against the seat. "So the bridesmaid who canceled on the bride at the last minute tried to message you yesterday about Bobby, the man Jared said was stalking Gabrielle?"

"Looks like it," Ophelia said.

Rocky woofed from the back seat, reminding him that they were just sitting in the vehicle and not going anywhere. Kyle started the engine. They pulled out of the driveway and started toward her home. "I'd honestly forgotten about Chloe. Gabrielle told me she was there the night she met Jared and that she knew Bobby was hassling her. But the fact that she didn't show up, because of some argument with Gabrielle, didn't seem suspicious to me and I didn't think it was a thread I needed to pull on."

"I honestly just assumed she'd had some spat with Gabrielle," Ophelia said. "I didn't imagine it had anything to do with Bobby."

This whole case was getting so wide and unwieldy, and he couldn't figure out what was actually connected to the death of John Doe and/or the RMK, and what wasn't. He'd started with one murdered body and since then questions had just continued to mount with no answers.

Who was John Doe and who'd killed him? The task force knew that the Rocky Mountain Killer was targeting men who'd been part of a nasty prank at a Young Rancher's Club dance ten years ago. But was John Doe connected to the YRC? Who was the masked man? Why did he shoot into the barn? Why did he break into Ophelia's home? How did Gabrielle's roommate Chloe and apparent stalker Bobby fit into all this?

He prayed to God for wisdom and thanked God for the incredible CSI sitting beside him.

"And everything was okay with your great-aunt?" he asked.

Ophelia groaned.

"I think something's bothering her," she said. "But when I tried to talk to her she just reminded me that it was important to be there for Jared on his big day. I don't know how I'm going to tell her I'm probably not going to be able to wear that purple dress."

"Did you tell her about the intruder?" Kyle asked. He turned onto her street.

"Yes, but I played it down," Ophelia said. "I never want to disappoint her. She was so good to me growing up, despite our differences. And like I told you, she asked me to invite you to the wedding tonight, as my date." She hesitated over the last word. "Look, to be incredibly honest, I told her we were just friends, but she jumped to the conclusion that either we were a romantic couple or she could somehow shoehorn us into being one by sheer will. It's like the only thing she thinks matters in my life is whether or not I've got a wedding date."

Which could be actually helpful, Kyle thought, if it allowed him to move freely through the wedding guests, gathering data while also essentially being undercover.

Her house came into view and Kyle silently thanked God to see the front light was shining. Both of her flat tires had been fixed, too. He pulled to a stop a few feet from the house and heard Ophelia shudder a breath. Instinctively, he reached for her hand and enveloped it in his.

"I'm fine," she said, like she was trying to reassure herself. "I was just suddenly hit by a visceral memory of what happened here last night."

"Hey." Kyle squeezed her hand and she squeezed it back.

"You're strong and you're going to get through this. But it's also okay to feel fear, anger or whatever else is washing over you right now. Trust me, I've felt every bad feeling in the book and it didn't make me any less of an FBI agent. Sometimes life's just lousy."

"Thank you," she whispered.

She leaned against his shoulder. He pulled his hand from hers and wrapped one arm around her, pulling her close into his side.

Suddenly, Rocky let out a sharp and urgent bark from the back seat. Kyle and Ophelia jumped apart. Kyle turned back. His partner was sitting up alert. The hackles rose at the back of Rocky's neck.

"Everything okay?" Ophelia asked.

"No," Kyle said. Chills ran down his spine. "I think he detects something."

Kyle cut the engine, they got out and then he opened the door for Rocky. The dog leaped out. Rocky sniffed the air toward the house. His growling grew louder.

"What does this mean?" Ophelia asked.

"Nothing good," Kyle said. His dog was only trained to detect one thing—death. Yet, in all the confusion and urgency of everything that had happened the night before, Kyle had dismissed how much Rocky had been barking and snarling, and how determined his partner had been to let Kyle know that something was wrong.

"Does he detect something in my house?" Ophelia asked.

"I think so," Kyle said. "Stay behind me, okay?" Then without waiting for Ophelia to answer, he looked down at his partner. "Show me."

The dog woofed and ran toward Ophelia's house, while Kyle and Ophelia ran after him. Rocky reached the front door, paused and looked back, waiting for his partner to catch up. Together they stepped into the house.

"Kyle West, FBI!" he called. "If there's anyone in here, identify yourself now."

No answer.

Okay, time to see what his partner was trying to tell him.

"Go on," Kyle told him.

Immediately, Rocky dashed across the living room, to where the basement door stood ajar. He nudged it open with his nose and ran down the stairs.

"Stay at the top of the stairs," Kyle told Ophelia. "I'm going down."

She nodded. Her eyes closed and her mouth moved, in what he somehow knew was silent prayer.

He switched on the light, pulled his weapon and started down the stairs. Rocky's growls grew until the whole house seemed to reverberate with the sound.

The basement was small and unfinished. With a plain concrete floor and sheets of plastic covering the pink insulation walls.

Rocky whimpered and pawed a spot on the far side of the wall. Kyle ran his hand over the dog's head.

"Good dog," he said softly. He ran his hand down the dog's side.

Kyle peeled the insulation back. A moment later he saw what the masked man had tried to stash behind it. It was a large, purple suitcase. He unzipped it and the smell of death filled his lungs.

The victim was female, with long red hair and her body curled peacefully into a ball, almost as if she'd fallen asleep, except for the single gunshot to the chest. The remnants of a broken golden locket hung around her neck, as if her killer had snapped the front half of it off.

His heart lurched as he silently prayed for justice.

"It's Chloe, isn't it?" Ophelia's voice came from behind him. Kyle turned and saw her standing in the basement, and while sorrow filled Ophelia's gaze, a fierce determination burned there, too. "She's the one who tried to warn me."

SEVEN

Law enforcement arrived mercifully quickly. Ophelia stood on her own lawn and watched as her home was declared a crime scene.

Detective Patricia Gonzales, one of the most senior investigators within the Santa Fe PD, oversaw the scene personally. She was an excellent officer, strong and reassuring, and someone who Ophelia had always felt proud working with. Patricia calmly reassured Ophelia that the Santa Fe PD would do everything in their power to make sure those behind the murder would be brought to justice. Ophelia felt her jaw clench so tightly it ached and watched as law enforcement and paramedics went in and out of her house. Despite the warm June air, her arms felt so cold they were almost numb. She wrapped them around herself like a shield and tried to pray but didn't even know how to put words to what she was feeling.

She heard the jingle of dog tags and looked up to see Kyle and Rocky coming toward her.

"You okay?" Kyle asked. "I know it can't be easy to see something like that."

His hand reached out and touched the small of her back. It was warm, strong and comforting, and part of her wanted very much to just relax into his touch. But instead she pulled away, feeling the need to stand on her own.

"I'm used to seeing dead bodies and crime scenes," she said. "I'm a professional. This is what I do. What I'm not used to is standing outside a crime scene feeling absolutely powerless, because, for reasons I have absolutely no control over, the crime scene is my house and the crime somehow has something to do with me."

Rocky butted his head up against her leg, as if to reassure her. She ran her hand over his silky ears and the K-9 licked her fingers.

"I'm sorry," she went on. "I don't how to explain it. I just feel so frustrated I can't tell if I want to shout or cry."

"I felt something like that when my brother and sister-in-law died," Kyle said, "and when I got the news my father had passed away. I wanted to be in the thick of it, doing something, even if there was nothing I could do."

He closed his eyes for a moment, and she suspected he was praying. Then he opened his eyes again and looked around. She followed his gaze. A news van was pulling up the street.

"Patricia!" Kyle called as he jogged over to the detective. Rocky and Ophelia followed. "How long can you keep the victim's name out of the press?"

"We don't have a firm identification yet," Patricia said, "but a wallet and phone were found on the body, so we're pretty certain this is Chloe Madison. But I need to contact the family before news gets out, so they don't find out online before they hear it from us."

"Can you give us an hour?" Kyle asked.

"I'll do my best," the detective said. "And just to clarify, neither of you are authorized to tell anyone that we believe Chloe is deceased or even mention that we found a body until we've notified her family. After that, I need you to limit the details to what's officially reported to the press, so that we limit false tips in the investigation. We really take doing things the right way and notifying next of kin seriously."

"Sounds good." Kyle turned to Ophelia and gestured to his vehicle. She nodded. He signaled Rocky to his side and the three of them started toward it. She didn't know what Kyle's plan was, but she trusted him and it wasn't like standing there watching law enforcement go in and out of her house was going to accomplish anything.

"What are you thinking?" Ophelia asked.

"That we have a very small window of time before everyone in the wedding party finds out Chloe was murdered," he said. His pace quickened. "And in my experience, as an investigator, a lot of people change their tune about a person once they discover they're gone."

"Because they don't want to speak ill of the dead," Ophelia said. "Or they don't want to look like a suspect."

"Exactly," Kyle said. "I want to go try interviewing your cousin and his fiancée again and see if we can get to the bottom of what was really going on with Chloe and Gabrielle's stalker, Bobby. My fear is that they're still going to refuse to talk to police and give us a straight answer."

"Yeah, I agree with you on that," Ophelia said. Rightly or wrongly, Jared wanted to protect his soon-to-be bride, and Gabrielle didn't trust the police. Ophelia worried both of them were too focused on the wrong priorities. Besides, Patricia had specifically told them they didn't have authorization to tell them anything about Chloe until a final determination was made and next of kin was notified. "I do think that once they know Chloe's dead, they're not going to give you a straight answer." When they reached his SUV, he opened the passenger door for her and she got inside. Rocky leaped in the back. "So, what's the plan?"

"You said Gabrielle and Jared are at the ranch trying to sort their wedding plans," he said. "I suggest we swing by and see if we can get them to talk to us." He swallowed hard. "They think I'm your wedding date, right?"

"Evelyn said she was going to tell them that," Ophelia confirmed.

"Well, if you're okay with letting them think we're there as a bridesmaid and her date, instead of investigators, I think that would be helpful." He glanced at her sideways. "If that's okay with you. I don't want to ask you to do anything you're not comfortable with."

"It's cool," Ophelia said. After all, it was not like she was going to be able to stop her family from jumping to conclusions anyway. Kyle could've shown up wearing a flashing neon sign proclaiming he and Ophelia were only friends, and they'd still insist on matchmaking them. "Let's go talk to them and see what they say."

At the end of the day, all she was doing was gathering evidence with an open mind, which was what she'd promised to do. If Jared was innocent of all this, as she was certain he was, she had every confidence Kyle would uncover that.

A few minutes later the beautiful adobe buildings of Santa Fe were in the rearview mirror, as they drove up the winding mountain roads back to Cherish Ranch. Kyle had slid on a pair of mirrored sunglasses to protect against the New Mexico sun as it rose higher in the sky and she could see the beautiful orange rock of the Sangre de Cristo Mountains reflected in their gaze. He rolled the windows down and let the warm and sweet June air move through the truck. She glanced in the side mirror and watched as Rocky stuck his head out the window. The K-9's long, silky ears flapped in the wind. Ophelia leaned back against the seat and prayed, feeling that same unusual peace that had filled her heart back in Kyle's home move through her again.

How could such incredible peace, faith and even joy coexist in a place of pain, worry and fear?

"Do you know what Evelyn told Jared and Gabrielle about us?" Kyle asked. The truck slowed as he neared the ranch. "Obviously, they all know I'm an FBI agent and you're a CSI, but I mean our relationship beyond that."

"You mean about being my wedding date?" Ophelia said. "I'm not sure exactly. But my great-aunt referred to you as my 'gentleman friend.'"

Kyle snorted, then wiped his eyes. "I've never even heard that expression before!"

"I'm glad one of us finds it funny," she said. "But then I'd hate being reduced to being seen as someone's date, and not a person in my own right. I work with an amazing group of people. But I can't tell you how many times I walked into a lab or crime scene during my training and some stranger assumed I wasn't a real tech and just somebody's girlfriend."

"True," Kyle said. Not that everyone wouldn't know he was law enforcement. "This is a first for me. I've never been anyone's wedding date. But I'll take whatever advantage I can get to solve these crimes."

The signs for Cherish Ranch and the petting zoo loomed ahead. He turned toward the ranch.

"Don't get me wrong," Ophelia said. "I know my family

loves me. I just wish the things they liked about me were the same things that I like about me."

"I get that," Kyle said. "You know I told you that my brother was my hero? I also wish he'd understood how hard it was for me sometimes to live in his shadow. He used to tease me, a lot. Especially when he got better grades than me. We were both on the football team and he used to call me 'butterfingers' every time I dropped a pass. When I was a senior, Caitlyn asked me to be her lab partner, and I quickly found out the real reason was just because she had a crush on my brother and wanted me to introduce them. They told their story at the wedding and people laughed, in a good-natured way. But it still kind of stung. He never knew how to tell me he loved me without razzing me. Maybe that was a holdover from how our dad impacted me, but he's tease me and make these jokes at my expense that weren't really funny. It wasn't until I read what they'd written about me in their will, and the fact that they wanted me to adopt Brody, that I had any idea of the good things they thought about me."

He pulled into the parking lot and stopped.

"Again," he said, "our dad was a really nasty jerk and we both dealt with it in our own very different ways."

"Families can be complicated," Ophelia said.

He sighed. "Yeah."

They got out of his vehicle and started toward the main building. Any worries she had that it might take a moment to locate Gabrielle and Jared vanished as they started up the steps and heard a babble of voices rising from the courtyard. Kyle clipped Rocky's leash on, and the three of them followed the sound.

They found Gabrielle and two members of the wedding

party, whom she vaguely recognized as Nolan and Lexi, standing in the courtyard, discussing the logistics of tables and food stations with two harried looking staff, while a middle-aged photographer set up a station for photographs.

"Ophelia! Kyle!" Gabrielle called. "I'm glad you made it!" Gabrielle smiled widely and ran across the courtyard toward them. She threw her arms around Ophelia and hugged her tightly, then quickly hugged Kyle as well. "I am so happy to see a friendly face. I'm sure Jared will be thrilled to see you, too. He's just in the office trying to talk some sense into the manager. A bunch of the wedding guests have canceled and the ranch won't let us use the barn because they say it's still an active crime scene, which I'm sure it's not, is it?"

"Well, you'd have to talk to the Santa Fe PD about that," Kyle said.

"But you can ask them about that, right?" Gabrielle asked. "Or at least get the police to tell people there's no reason to think that murder had anything to do with my wedding?"

"I'd be happy to personally talk to anybody who had concerns," Kyle said. He pushed his sunglasses up onto the top of his head, and Ophelia noticed he manage to sound reassuring while completely sidestepping what she was asking. "If any of your guests or wedding party have any thoughts about what happened yesterday you can send them to me."

Gabrielle stepped back. "It's wonderful to see you two together. And, Ophelia, I just wish you'd told me yesterday that you and this hunky cop were an item!"

"I'm actually an FBI Agent. And," Kyle added with a wide grin, "in Ophelia's defense, we really haven't put a label on anything. And the last thing Ophelia wanted was to draw any attention away from you two on your big day."

Wow, he was good at this. As opposed to her, yesterday, when she'd been asked to fill in for Chloe as a bridesmaid, and Ophelia had felt like every word out of her mouth was awkward and wrong. Then her heart sank as she remembered what had happened to Chloe. Gabrielle and Jared were like a pair of stubborn deer in headlights refusing to admit the fact that the next car on the road could be headed their way.

Lord, please help us protect Gabrielle and everyone else who might be in this killer's sights.

"You two are such sweeties," Gabrielle said. Then she crouched down and looked at Rocky. "Not to mention you are so adorable you can take the attention away from anyone! Do you think you'd be willing to carry a little basket of flowers down the aisle for me?"

Gabrielle glanced at Kyle hopefully. Ophelia watched as Kyle pressed his lips tightly together and looked like he was fighting the urge to laugh.

"I'm so sorry," he said. "He doesn't really do tricks."

"Such a shame," Gabrielle said. She turned and waved at the gray-haired man with the camera. "Hey, photographer! Get over here and get a picture of these two to update our wedding's social media page."

"Absolutely," Kyle said gamely. "Sounds like a plan."

Anything, Ophelia imagined, to increase the likelihood people would have candid conversations with him later. The photographer waved them in front of a row of flowering rosebushes and instructed them to put their arms together and turn to face the camera. She slid her arms around Kyle's neck as directed and felt his strong hands tighten around her waist. Rocky sat tall on the ground in front of them. The photographer started clicking. Ophelia tried to smile naturally and face the lens, hoping she didn't look anywhere near as awkward as she felt.

"Now if you could give her a quick kiss on the cheek for this next one," the photographer said.

Kyle's lips brushed lightly against her cheekbones just below her temple, sending an unexpected tingle of electricity through her skin.

Instinctively she turned toward him, and for one fleeting moment their lips met in a kiss.

EIGHT

Kyle stepped back and his eyes widened. She stepped back, too, heat rising to her face. She wanted to apologize, tell him that it was an accident and that she hadn't meant to kiss him. But the truth was she wasn't even sure which one had kissed the other first.

Kyle ran his hand over the back of his neck.

"Good, good," the photographer said and looked down at the screen as if confirming he had gotten the shots. "Now, can somebody show me where the actual ceremony will be tonight?"

"Nolan can." Gabrielle gestured to the black-haired groomsman, who was still standing at the other side of the courtyard with the bridesmaid and ranch staff. "And actually, Lexi, can you go find Jared and let him know Ophelia and her boyfriend the cop are here?"

He's an agent, not a cop, and he's not my boyfriend.

Lexi disappeared into the main ranch and within moments Jared came out, alone. He looked stressed, harried and not at all like a man who was about to marry the love of his life. But while he said hello to Ophelia and Kyle, he made a beeline straight for Gabrielle and wrapped his arm around her shoulder.

"They said we could still have the wedding in the outdoor chapel as planned," he said. "But they're insisting we hold the reception in the courtyard. Apparently they hold beautiful receptions out there all the time. It's just that after the problem with our payment going through yesterday, thanks to Gabrielle's parents being delayed, they're not being as sympathetic as they could to the fact that all we want is to get married."

"Have you considered relocating the wedding somewhere more private and quieter?" Kyle asked. "Or even eloping?"

The federal agent was still smiling, with that easygoing grin. But there was a firmer edge to his voice now. Was it because the four of them were alone? She couldn't imagine that the kiss had rattled him, too.

"We'll be fine," Jared said firmly. He stepped up and put his arm around Gabrielle's shoulder. "We actually talked in great length last night about the Bobby situation. While she eventually agreed it was right that I told you, we also decided that as long as we stayed together, we'll be fine. He's not about to make an attempt to hurt to Gabrielle while I'm around."

But what about everyone else who wasn't them?

"Whatever's going on, I think it's bigger than just one body in the barn," Ophelia said. She felt like she was walking a tightrope between what she was allowed to tell them and the fact that she didn't want her cousin to do anything that put himself, his fiancée, her great-aunt, and a bunch of friends and family in danger. "Look, somebody broke into my house last night."

Gabrielle gasped. Her hands rose to her lips.

"Are you serious?" Jared stepped toward her. "Are you okay?"

"I'm fine," she said quickly. "Kyle invited me to stay with him and his mother."

"Well, you do live in a lower income neighborhood," Jared said and Ophelia's fingers clenched. "I'm so sorry that happened. But I'm sure it's just a badly timed coincidence."

"There's more," Ophelia went on. "I also got a video message from Chloe saying she needed to talk to me about the whole Bobby situation."

She wasn't sure what kind of reaction she was getting to that. But suddenly Gabrielle's face paled and something like fear flickered through her gaze. Then the bride smiled firmly, reached out and looped her arm through Ophelia's.

"Okay, I think it's time you and I had some girl talk," Gabrielle said firmly. "No guys. Just us. It's clear that my fiancé got you worried. And so I guess it's time I tell you what's really going on."

Ophelia glanced at Kyle. She couldn't just go off and talk to Gabrielle about Bobby without him. He was the FBI agent and the expert in questioning suspects. Her home was in the lab. But to her surprise, Kyle waved his hand as if encouraging them to go.

"That sounds fantastic," Kyle said. "I'll appreciate the opportunity to get to know Jared better."

You've got this, his eyes added. But did she, though?

Either way, she let her cousin's fiancée walk her away down the beautifully overgrown garden path to a rustic wooden bench Ophelia imagined had appeared in a lot of people's pictures. They sat and only then did Gabrielle pull her arm out of Ophelia's. She turned to face her.

"First of all—" Gabrielle's eyes widened with sincerity

"—I need you to know that I really love your cousin and would do anything to make him happy. He's everything to me and I'm really sorry for all of this." Her manicured hands swung wide as if encompassing an invisible ball of chaos. "Chloe is my former roommate and I love her. But she is also a total drama queen and busybody who spends all of her time stirring up trouble for other people. This whole situation with Bobby would never have gotten out of hand if it hadn't been for her.

"Okay," Gabrielle went on. "So, Chloe and I met Bobby in a hotel bar. She liked him, but he was only interested in me. As Jared told you, Bobby and I went on a couple of dates that didn't go anywhere. I tried to end it, he got really clingy and he didn't want to take no for an answer. He called and sent flowers. It was really annoying."

She blew out a long breath and rolled her eyes, as if she saw Bobby more like a persistent fly at a picnic than a potential serial killer.

"Chloe made it worse by trying to meddle in my business," Gabrielle added. "She would talk to him when he called and wanted to hear his side of the story. Maybe she was hoping that if she let him cry on her shoulder, he'd fall in love with her. Then she canceled on coming to my wedding. Maybe because of him, I don't know. I'm just really sorry that she tried to involve you in this nonsense."

Was that really what happened? Gabrielle sounded like she actually believed what she was saying, yet Ophelia wasn't sure if it was true.

But before she could even ask a question, she heard the sound of Jared, Kyle and Rocky running down the path toward them. Ophelia leaped to her feet. Gabrielle did, too.

"Gabrielle, baby!" Jared stretched out both hands toward his fiancée, as if she was about to fall from a great height and he was preparing to catch her. "Chloe's dead!"

"What?" Gabrielle's voice broke.

"It was leaked to the news," Kyle said softly, as he stepped to Ophelia's side.

Ophelia reached out a hand toward Gabrielle to comfort her. But instead, she watched as Gabrielle tumbled into Jared's arms, in a flurry of sobs and questions. He ran his hand over her back, soothing and comforting her. Then her cousin fixed his eyes on Ophelia. And a colder look than she'd ever seen before filled his steely blue gaze.

"I think you should leave," Jared said. He glanced coolly from her to Kyle. "Both of you. I know you must've known something about this before you showed up here today, and yet neither of you told us anything."

Gabrielle still sobbed into his shoulder.

"I'm sorry." Ophelia's heart lurched. She took a step toward them. "All I knew was that a woman's body had been found. We didn't have a positive ID and we weren't authorized to tell you anything about it."

"Can't you talk like a normal person for once?" Jared's voice rose. She stepped back as if his words had literally slapped her. "I get that your sad little life is all about work, and you don't really click with people like Gabrielle and me, and our friends. And I've never given you a hard time for that. But I don't care that you didn't have a positive ID, or you weren't authorized or whatever. You still should've told me about Chloe and everything you know about this case. I'm your cousin!"

The words "I'm sorry" still floated on her tongue. But what was she apologizing for? For being driven? For doing her job? For putting her career above the fact that her cousin wanted an inside track on the investigation?

"Look, I tried to tell Grandma Evelyn that it was a mistake to have you in the wedding party." Jared blew out a hard breath. "It would break her heart if you didn't come to the wedding. Just please, leave and stay out of our way tonight. I'll tell Grandma you didn't feel up to being in the wedding."

He turned his back on her and started down the path, with his arm still around Gabrielle.

Ophelia wanted to run after him, apologize again, do or say something to make it right.

But instead, she felt Kyle's hand brush against her elbow on one side and Rocky's head press against the back of her leg on the other, as if they were working together to lead her back to the truck.

The three of them walked to the truck in silence and got inside. They'd already pulled out, left the ranch and driven a few miles down the highway before Kyle spoke. "You okay? That was pretty harsh."

"I don't know," Ophelia admitted. "He's never raised his voice at me like that before."

"He's scared, frustrated and angry," Kyle said. "He's probably used to being in control of things and is lashing out because things aren't going his way."

"Gabrielle spun this whole story that matches all the facts we've heard before," Ophelia said. "Only she said that Chloe kept trying to get in the middle of her and Bobby. Gabrielle said she blamed the whole Bobby mess on the fact that Chloe kept stirring up drama. I definitely can't imagine her saying any of that now that she knows Chloe's dead."

"When you two stepped away to talk, Jared asked if I

could give him the inside track on the RMK case," Kyle said, "and tell him some of the details that investigators haven't told the public," Kyle said. "He also asked if there was anything I could do to speed up the Cherish Ranch investigation. It became clear to me pretty quickly that he expected some kind of preferential treatment from the police that he was frustrated he wasn't getting."

He rested his left arm on the window and his right hand on the steering wheel.

"I'm not justifying what he said, but I do understand how powerless and frustrated he must feel. I know how hard it felt for me when my colleagues knew that my father had passed away due a self-inflicted gunshot wound before I was told. Or that my brother and Caitlyn didn't survive the crash. In both cases, all they would tell me was that something had had happened and someone would brief me at the hospital. Again, I'm not saying this reaction was either right or fair. Just that I hope you can find a way to forgive him."

She tried to respond, but realized she couldn't find the right words to say. So she just closed her eyes instead and prayed the same words she felt like she'd been praying over and over again for almost twenty-four hours. She asked God for mercy, justice, guidance, compassion, wisdom and help.

When she opened her eyes and turned to Kyle again, he was watching the rearview mirror.

She followed his gaze. For a long moment she saw nothing but the empty mountain road behind them. Then a blue truck appeared over the horizon, its bright chrome almost glimmering in the hot New Mexico sun. A man in a cowboy hat sat at the wheel.

"Everything okay?" she asked.

"No," Kyle said. "This blue truck and I have been playing peekaboo for the last five minutes, no matter how many turns I take. Looks like we're being followed again. But I'm not going to run. It's time we make a stand and fight."

Kyle had always found something both majestic and intimidating about how the Rocky Mountains towered over the outskirts of Santa Fe, where tall trees, scorching deserts, red buttes and sandstone structures all coexisted in an unbelievably beautiful harmony.

It was the last he was scanning for now.

Twisted and intricate, the pale beige structures rose from the earth like giant versions of a child's sandcastles, arches and towers now frozen in time.

Well, a fortress was what he needed now.

He urged the SUV faster until the truck disappeared from view again, while his eyes continued to survey the row ahead.

"I'm looking for a place to pull over," he said. But even as the words left his mouth, he saw the trio of naturally formed sculptures, each taller than a house, standing tall like a queen with her two ladies in waiting, light brown against the darker red and orange rock surrounding them.

He took one more glance to the rearview mirror. The truck had vanished from view temporarily. He prayed he'd have enough time to do what he needed before the truck caught up with him again. Then he looked at Ophelia. Her eyes were closed and it looked like she was praying.

"Okay, so here's the plan," he said. "See those three tall rock sculptures ahead?" She opened her eyes and nodded. "In a minute I'm going to quickly stop the vehicle and hop out. I'll pop the hood to make it look like I'm having engine trouble." He glanced at her face. "I want you to stay in the vehicle."

"Alone?"

"You'll be much safer there than you will be outside," he said. "The windows are bulletproof and the walls are reinforced. Just stay low and if anything goes wrong dial 911."

"And where will you be?"

"Out there," he said. "Taking him down before he can get to you."

He watched as fear and courage battled in the depths of her beautiful blue eyes. Immediately he switched the hand that was holding the steering wheel, so he could take her hand and hold it.

"I trust you," she said.

And despite the hundreds, maybe thousands, of times he'd heard those words in his life, somehow as they flew out of Ophelia's mouth, they hit him deep inside his core in a way they never had before.

Help me, Lord. I don't want to let her down.

He pulled his hands from hers and steered rapidly off the road, in between the first handmaiden rock and the queen. He popped the hood, leaped out and was about to open the door for Rocky to join him, when the dog's large eyes met his through the window. Instead, Kyle swallowed hard and closed the driver's-side door.

"Rocky, stay with Ophelia," he said. "Guard her and keep her safe."

The dog woofed softly.

Kyle had barely managed to duck behind the sculpture he thought of as the queen when he saw the truck appear on the horizon. He pressed his back into the sandstone crevasses and hoped that the man in the cowboy hat would take the bait.

The truck drew closer and closer. Kyle held his breath and prayed. He watched as the brake lights flashed. The cowboy pulled to a stop a few yards away from Kyle's SUV. From what Kyle could see, there was just the driver in the car, no other passengers. The cowboy was tall and thin, with an expensive-looking hat pulled down over his eyes. The truck looked expensive, too, unlike the battered van and rusty car he'd seen the masked man use before.

The cowboy got out slowly and began to walk toward Kyle's SUV.

He wasn't limping. This wasn't the same man Kyle had clipped in the calf. Kyle tracked his steps as he grew closer. Thirty paces, twenty paces, ten…

"FBI! Get down on the ground with your hands up!"

Kyle leaped from behind his hiding spot. The man turned to run. Kyle was faster. He tackled him, bringing him down to the ground and deftly cuffing his hands behind his back.

"Don't shoot!" the young man yelped. The hat fell from his head showing short black hair beneath. "I'm not the killer. I promise!"

The voice was familiar. But Kyle couldn't place it straight away. He stepped back enough to let the man turn over.

It was Nolan.

The groomsman he'd seen back at the ranch, showing the photographer where the outdoor wedding chapel was. And also, the man who'd been with Gabrielle when John Doe was killed.

Unless she'd lied to give him an alibi.

Kyle stepped back to let the man breathe, but kept his eyes locked on his face and his hand at the ready should he need to pull out his weapon.

"Why were you following me?"

"I…I was trying to catch up with you to help you," Nolan spluttered.

Kyle looked the young man over. Every single item of

clothing he was wearing cost more than Kyle made in a month and his eyes were darting every possible direction without meeting Kyle's eyes.

"I don't believe you," Kyle said, "because if you had been, you wouldn't have kept pulling back and slowing down like that every time I slowed down. You were following me and I'm not interested in playing guessing games about why. Two people associated with a wedding you're a groomsman in have been killed in the past twenty-four hours. And it's possible those murders are linked to the Rocky Mountain Killer who's murdered another six people across mountain country. So I suggest you spend the ride to the police station thinking hard about telling me the truth." He hauled Nolan up to his feet and prepared to steer him toward his SUV. "Don't worry, we'll get someone to come and pick up your truck."

He turned toward Ophelia. Rocky had climbed into the driver's seat to join her. They were both watching him.

"Call 911 and tell them I need backup," he called. "I've got a GPS tracker in my SUV. They can lock on the location."

"On it!" Ophelia said. He watched as she placed the call.

He had a cage divider he could raise in the back of the SUV, between the front and back seats, but he'd rather not drive a potential serial killer back to town with Ophelia and Rocky in the SUV.

"No, wait!" Nolan yelled. "All right, I was following you. But only because I saw a man put something in your SUV!"

Kyle stopped. Instinctively, his eyes locked where he'd left Rocky and Ophelia. The dog had climbed into the driver's seat. Ophelia had the phone to her ear and was saying something to someone, likely dispatch, but her eyes were tracking him through the rearview mirror. "You saw some-one put something in my vehicle?"

"Maybe, I don't know." Nolan said. He was probably only six or seven years younger than Kyle, but it felt more like fifteen or twenty. "When I came back from showing the photographer the outdoor chapel, I saw this big guy crouched down beside your SUV."

"Where exactly? Which side of the vehicle?"

"Back door, passenger side, I think," Nolan said. He didn't sound certain. "I didn't think anything at first. But then I remembered that I heard the RMK liked to taunt po-lice with clues and messages. And I thought if I could get what was left in your vehicle, I could figure out who the killer was and maybe get some reward money or something."

"Did he have a limp?" Kyle asked.

"I think so, maybe."

Kyle blew out a frustrated breath. He believed him. The story was too ridiculous to be invented.

"Good news," Ophelia called. She got out of the vehicle and Rocky bounded out after her. "Backup is eight minutes out. Some campers got into a fight and started a fire west of here, so emergency vehicles were already in the area."

Kyle thanked God for that.

"He says he was only following us because he thought someone might've tried to plant something in my vehicle," he called back.

"What kind of something?" Ophelia asked.

"I don't know, but he says it might be in the back seat."

She opened the back door, bent down and looked for a long moment. Then she checked the front seats.

"I don't see anything," she said.

"I'm not lying," Nolan stammered.

Ophelia looked around the outside of the vehicle. Her

phone was still in her hand. Rocky sat on the ground and looked at her thoughtfully.

"Wait," she said. "There's something sticking out of the gas tank. Like a piece of string. Maybe it's a fuse, but if so it's a clumsy design because the gas tank didn't detonate."

"Don't touch it!" Kyle called.

"I won't," she said. "Thankfully law enforcement are already on their way." She closed the passenger-side door. Kyle heard a loud and metallic click. She looked up and her face paled. "It slipped inside the tank."

"Run!"

Oh, Lord...please help us.

Ophelia and Rocky both turned and ran toward him. Behind him he could hear Nolan making tracks and hoped the young man would make it out of the blast zone. But Kyle ran toward Ophelia.

He had to get to her. He had to make sure she was okay.

In an instant, Rocky had reached his side. Silently, Kyle signaled him to keep running.

"Kyle!" Ophelia shouted. "Run!"

Not yet. Not without her.

But she was only steps away from him now. He reached out his hand to grab hers. She reached out for him.

And then his truck exploded.

NINE

In an instant he watched, helpless, as a wall of orange flame rushed toward Ophelia's body. Then the force of the blast lifted her off the ground and hurled her through the air toward him. Kyle caught her with both arms and held on tight, as he felt himself tossed backward through the air. For a moment he felt powerless to do anything but grasp Ophelia to him with all his might, willing himself not to let her go. Then he hit the ground, shoulder first, and rolled over and over again on the rough ground, absorbing the impact of the blast in his body and sheltering her with his arms.

Finally, his body shuddered to a stop and he felt Ophelia slip from his arms. For a moment he lay there on the ground as soot and ash rained down around him. He looked up to see a ball of orange flame where his SUV has been. Then he felt Ophelia's hand grab his and pull him up, and he climbed to his feet.

"You saved me." She threw her arms around his neck, with such force that for a moment he thought he was going to lose his balance and fall back down again.

Of course, I saved you. I couldn't just leave you.

He wanted to tell her how relieved he was that she was

okay and promise he'd never let anything hurt her. But the words died on his tongue as hot, smoky air seared his lungs.

Instead, he wrapped his arms around her waist and kissed her—or maybe she kissed him first, he didn't know. All he knew was that as their lips met he felt like it was the first real kiss he'd ever had in his life. The first one that ever had a hope of meaning all the things a kiss was supposed to mean.

Then she pulled out of his arms and it was like all of his other senses suddenly came alive and rushed back in to fill the space she'd left. He could hear the sound of Rocky barking and sirens blaring in the distance. He could feel the heat on his skin and smell the acrid scent of burning rubber. Ophelia ran toward Nolan and Rocky. Kyle followed, and as he reached his partner, he felt Rocky nuzzle his hand in greeting.

He uncuffed Nolan. The man seemed too shaken and thankful to be alive to run, and truth was Kyle knew that regardless of why Nolan had tried to follow him, he was also the reason they were all alive now. Kyle then watched as a cavalcade of police, firefighters and ambulances crossed the horizon toward them. Within moments, the sound of sirens, shouting and emergency personnel pouring from their vehicles had completely overtaken the air.

"I need to take Nolan in for questioning," he told Ophelia. "I want you to come with me and observe via the two-way mirror. There might be things you pick up because of your connection to Jared and Gabrielle."

But instead, Ophelia shook her head.

"I'm going to get someone to take me to the lab," she said. "I need to check in on how far the team has gotten in processing everything that we collected yesterday. Obviously, I won't be able to process anything found in my own house. But I can at least give Isla an update on everything we found in relation to the death of John Doe. I still haven't forgotten about that cuff link."

He opened his mouth to try to convince her that they should head back to Santa Fe together and wasn't even sure what he was going to say, when she raised her hand to stop him.

"Kyle, I need to go do my job."

He nodded. "Okay, I get it."

She bent down and hugged Rocky, nuzzling her face against the dog's snout. Then she turned and ran toward a Santa Fe PD officer. Still, part of him was expecting he'd talk to her again before she left the scene. But instead, when the flames were extinguished and the swell of response vehicles began to recede, Kyle looked around to realize that Ophelia had left without him realizing it. Rocky whimpered and sniffed the air as if he too realized that something was missing and was offering to help Kyle search for it.

"It's okay, buddy," Kyle said. "Ophelia just had to go back to work."

After all, he wasn't actually her wedding date or her partner; they were just two professionals who happened to get thrown together over one particular crime scene and might never be again.

Thankfully, Nolan quickly agreed to come in for questioning, which spared Kyle having to jump through the hoops of an arrest. Despite the fact that the incident started with Nolan following an FBI agent's SUV—and that SUV then exploding—it wasn't entirely clear what crime Nolan had actually committed.

The local FBI field office was small and not set up for questioning suspects, but Patricia had gotten an officer to drive Kyle, Rocky and Nolan to the central police station, and gave Kyle use of an interrogation room. There, Kyle and Nolan sat across from each other in the plain rectangular space with gray walls, while Rocky lay by Kyle's feet, and Nolan worried the plastic cup of water he'd been given and repeated multiple versions of the exact same story he'd told Kyle back when he'd first had handcuffs on.

"Where did you even get the idea that the Rocky Mountain Killer would plant evidence in my vehicle?" he asked.

"Because that's all everyone is talking about!" Nolan said. "If anyone tells you they're not talking about the RMK they're lying. It's all over social media." And Kyle expected that a lot of what people were talking about was either untrue or wild speculation. "But I've never been to Elk Lake or whatever it's called, or been part of anything called the Young Rancher's Club, and I don't know anyone who has."

"Are you aware that Gabrielle gave you an alibi for the time when John Doe was killed in the barn yesterday?" Kyle asked.

"Yeah." He nodded. "We ran into each other in the outdoor chapel area and talked about the weather."

His gaze darted toward the ceiling. He still wasn't being completely honest about something, but Kyle wasn't sure what.

"Nolan." Kyle leaned forward. "Is there something going on between you and Gabrielle? Some reason why she'd lie for you?"

"No!" The plastic cup crunched in Nolan's hands. "I'm not like that. I'd never mess with my friend's fiancée. She really, really loves Jared. Like a lot. And wants to marry him."

A swift knock sounded on the door. Kyle stood, and so did Rocky, and they walked to the door. It was detective Patricia Gonzales.

He and Rocky stepped outside to join her in the hallway and closed the door behind them.

"What are we looking at in terms of charges?" she asked.

He pressed his tongue against his gums. Local Santa Fe PD had a completely different jurisdictional authority than he did. For example, while he could charge people with felonies, he couldn't give anyone a traffic ticket or ding them for running a stop sign. That was the role of the local police he was cooperating with on this case.

However, when it came to Nolan, there wasn't really anything there that was chargeable.

"He's got no record," Kyle said, "and I didn't witness him commit a crime. I could charge him with resisting arrest or attempting to tamper with evidence, but it's a stretch."

"So we let him go?" Patricia asked. "Or do we hold him and hope we get something more?"

"I think we let him go," Kyle said. "As much as I'd like to hold him, I've also got to think about the fact that if I do that nobody in that wedding party is going to speak to me about anything, and I don't even know if this guy is guilty of anything except being foolish. I think our best move is to thank him, treat him like a helpful witness, and apologize for any inconvenience and give him a ride wherever he wants. Make him think we like him."

"But we keep an eye on him?" Patricia asked.

"We keep an eye on the whole wedding party."

A uniformed cop came down the hallway.

"Agent West?" he said. "There's someone at the front desk wanting to speak to you, Should I show her to a room?"

Hope floated in his chest. Was it Ophelia?

"You go," Patricia said dryly. "I'll go thank our witness for his cooperation and tell him how much we appreciate his help."

Kyle walked down the maze of hallways back to the front desk. As he turned a corner he saw MCK9 Task Force member Meadow Ames striding toward him, with Grace by her side. Incredibly athletic, with long dark hair and bright green eyes, Meadow exuded a special combination of determination and sense of adventure that seemed to match perfectly with her K-9 partner, who specialized in both tracking and search and rescue. Kyle privately thought he'd never seen a human and K-9 partner match so perfectly.

"You made it!" He clasped her on her shoulder as the dogs wagged tails at each other in greeting. "It's good to see you."

"It's good to see you, too." Meadow smiled, but genuine concern moved through the depths of her eyes. Together they walked out of the Santa Fe PD office, along with their K-9 partners. "I heard you got into some vehicle trouble today. Everything okay?"

"Everyone's okay, thankfully," he said. "Although my SUV has seen better days. Also, I know it probably seems minor in the whole scheme of things, but if you are going to be spending time with my mom on protective detail, can you try to find out why she's making so many trips to the pharmacy? I keep asking, but she won't tell me."

"Will do." Meadow nodded. "You know that Chase wants me to take your mom and Brody to a safe house. I get that you want to keep them close. But with the attack on Ophelia's home and now your vehicle, I think Chase is right that even if Grace and I are protecting them, as long as they're in your home they're in danger. At least until we figure out what's going on."

"I know." Kyle's eyes searched the bright blue sky above.

His brain knew that his boss was right and Meadow would keep his family safe. But still something in him ached. His job took him away from Brody too much as it was, and now his colleague was going to take Brody and Mom to a safe house.

Lord, I don't know to be both the family man and lawman you've called me to be. I feel like I'm failing at both. And now this case is taking my kid away from me. Please, open my eyes to the clues I need to see and help me solve this before anyone else gets hurt.

Including his own heart.

Ophelia felt a special type of joy fill her heart as she stepped through the familiar doors of the Santa Fe PD Crime Scene Unit's forensic lab. Thankfully, her car and home had finally both been cleared, so she was back in her own clothes and able to be at the wheel of her own vehicle. But even though she knew her boss would've let her take more time off despite the fact that the forensic lab was short-staffed, right now there was nowhere else she wanted to be.

She grabbed her white lab coat from her locker and slid it on, feeling the familiar crisp and clean fabric. Then she clipped on her identification pass and started for the lab. The memory of her two fleeting kisses with Kyle still buzzed on her lips and rattled in the back of her mind. The first had been an accident. But the second? That had been full of emotions she didn't even want to begin to analyze.

After all, it didn't matter what she felt about Kyle, or his son, and that wonderful little family who'd opened their home and lives to her when she'd needed someone. Kyle had made it clear that he wasn't interested in a relationship. And even if she did have time for one—which she didn't—it wasn't good for her to go chasing after a man who'd preemptively rejected the thought of starting a life with her. She needed to focus on the life she had, and the work she did, instead of worrying about a future that would never be hers.

The forensic lab was abuzz with colleagues in matching lab coats, each hard at work and focused on their own station as their eyes peered through goggles, glasses and microscopes at the evidence in front of them. When Ophelia crossed through the room to her desk, colleagues looked up and smiled. All of them had heard about the shooting at the ranch and the body found in her house. But while person after person asked how she was doing and offered to be there for her if she needed support, once she thanked them and reassured them that she was fine, each was quick to turn back to their tasks at hand. She appreciated that.

Lord, when I'm here I feel like myself. Like I'm doing what I'm meant to be doing. That I am doing the work You've called me to do. Thank You so much for that and that I get to be a part of this work.

Nobody here thought of her as a victim, although she knew for a fact most had processed the crime scenes in the barn and her house. And definitely nobody thought she was weird or unusual for spending her life working with what her great-aunt Evelyn would call "blood and guts."

But now, she had to buckle down and get to work.

Various white boards around the room listed the evidence and process of different open cases. As she'd told Kyle, there was a backlog. There was only so much hard work and overtime she could do to make up for the lab being short-staffed and overloaded. As much as she'd have hoped that everything that had been collected less than twenty-four hours ago at Cherish Ranch had been sorted, there were still a lot of white spaces on the board.

Based on what she could see, her dedicated colleagues had processed a whole lot of different DNA and blood samples, but only one DNA profile was found in the blood in the barn—the victim's. There hadn't been any unexpected DNA samples where Chloe's body had been found in Ophelia's basement, either. Seems whoever the masked man behind the crimes was, he'd been smart enough not to leave any DNA behind. Nothing unfamiliar or unexpected had been found in the remnants of the cleaning solution in the barn, either. Or in the white van.

So many tests had been run already with so few answers. However, in her line of work, often the sooner one eliminated the wrong things the faster they were able to determine the right ones.

Sure enough, a new lab laptop was waiting on her desk, to replace the one she'd lost the night before. Ophelia found the gold cuff link in the evidence locker and double-checked with the acting head of the lab that the blood sample on it had been tested and come back to the unknown victim. Okay, now to finally get a good look at the inscription on it.

She took it back to her workstation, slid on a fresh pair of rubber gloves, carefully retrieved the cuff link from the evidence bag with a pair of tweezers and dropped it in a beaker of cleaning solution. Tiny bubbles rose from the cuff link as the solution did its work.

Then she opened the new laptop and called Isla, the

MCK9 technical analyst. Within moments Isla's face appeared on the screen.

"Hey!" Isla said. "It's really good to see you. I heard you survived some pretty scary stuff this morning and I've been praying nonstop."

Genuine care and concern filled the tech's brown eyes, but there was a brightness to her smile, too. Ophelia instinctively liked her. The whole MCK9 Task Force seemed great, but something about Isla especially made Ophelia feel like they were on the same wavelength.

"I appreciate it," Ophelia said. "The discovery that the killer took a second life is really shocking and sad. I'm just glad everyone survived the SUV vehicle explosion."

Isla nodded. "Yeah, we've all been thanking God for that, and looking forward to getting to the bottom of this."

Ophelia quickly ran her through all the results the team had uncovered so far.

"The bullets found in our Joe Doe still haven't been tested against the other bullets in previous cases involving the RMK to see if they were fired from the same gun," Ophelia said. "Can you send me through a picture so I can try to match ballistics?"

"Absolutely," Isla said. "I'm on it."

The individual lines, ridges and groves that each gun left on the bullets it fired were as unique as fingerprints, allowing investigators to not just match them to the type of gun they were fired from, but the specific weapon itself. The bullets that killed all six of the RMK victims had been fired through the barrel of the exact same gun, though that gun had never been found. Had the bullets that killed John Doe come from that weapon, too?

Ophelia left the video call open. She got one of the bullets found in the barn from evidence, plucked it out of the small clear evidence box with a fresh pair of tweezers and then created a three-dimensional rendered model of it using the lab's high-tech camera. Slowly a detailed image of the bullet appeared on the screen in front of her as the camera did its work, like it was slowly being drawn by an invisible hand. The computer chimed, letting her know the render was complete. She sent it to Isla and a moment later Isla's own image of one of the RMK's bullets loaded onto the screen beside it.

Ophelia used the computer's track pad to rotate the images this way and that on the screen, trying to line up the striation lines on the two bullets to see if they'd been made by the same gun barrel. But no matter how patiently she maneuvered the two pictures, the rifling marks didn't line up.

"They're not a match," Isla said finally.

"No, they're not." Ophelia blew out a hard breath and leaned back in her chair. "These bullets were not fired from the same gun."

"Wow." Isla looked as shocked and disappointed by the news as Ophelia felt. "So the bullets that killed John Doe in the barn were not fired from the same gun that killed the RMK's six victims. Do you think we're looking at a copycat?"

"Maybe," Ophelia said. Did that mean that the murders of John Doe and Chloe Madison had nothing at all to do with the Rocky Mountain Killer? She glanced over at the beaker, where she'd placed the cuff link. It had stopped bubbling and the liquid was slightly cloudy. "One second. I'm about to have something else for you."

She pulled the cuff link from the cleaning solution. It glistened. Gold, she was sure, not some cheap knockoff. It was worth a good amount of money. The engraving was so stylized she couldn't make it out at first. So she set it directly in front of the 3D camera and started scanning it with the high-definition lens, allowing Isla to see it in real time along with her.

Slowly, the engraving came into view in large and magnified letters on the screen.

First an *R*, then a *W* and finally an *N*.

"So, *RWN*," Isla said. "Not *RMK*. I have no idea what that stands for."

"Neither do I." So first the bullets weren't a match and now the engraving on the cuff link turned out to be *RWN* and not *RMK*.

"It's looking less and less like the murders of John Doe and Chloe Madison have anything to do with the Rocky Mountain Killer case," Isla said.

"I'm sorry," Ophelia said. "I know you guys were hoping this could be a big break in catching the guy."

Kyle had definitely hoped it would be. Ophelia's cell phone rang. She glanced down at the screen. It was Jared. She wondered if he was calling to yell at her some more, apologize or pretend their entire conflict had never happened. Knowing Jared, it could be any of the above. And any which way, it could wait until she was finished with Isla. She sent the call through to voice mail.

"Hey," Isla said. "Look on the bright side. At least I now have a solid lead in finding out John Doe's identity. I'm going to go cross-check the picture of the cuff link with the work of jewelers in New Mexico, Wyoming and beyond. Hopefully I'll be able to track down the person who did this work and see if they have a record of who they sold it to."

"Try Nevada," Ophelia said. "That's where Bobby was

apparently from. And thanks so much. I appreciate your help."

"That's what we're here for," Isla said. "I'm going to fill the rest of the team in. Talk to you soon."

The call ended and Ophelia silently thanked God for her. The phone rang. Jared was calling again. Time she answered it.

"Hey," she said. "I'm at work."

"Gabrielle's gone!" His words came out in a panicked rush. "I think Bobby kidnapped her!"

TEN

"I'm on my way." Ophelia leaped to her feet. She closed her laptop, grabbed her bag and moved swiftly through the lab, without even stopping to take off her lab coat. "What happened?"

"When we got back to the hotel, we heard that Kyle's truck had caught fire and Nolan had been arrested," Jared said. He sounded so panicked it was like he was struggling to even breathe. "Gabrielle got all upset. She blamed me and said it was my fault for telling you about Bobby because you got the cops involved and made the drama even worse."

Ophelia didn't exactly see it that way. She reached the main hallway and started down the stairs to the parking lot, not bothering to wait for the elevator.

"She went into her hotel room," he continued. "After it was over an hour I got worried and went to check on her. But she was gone."

So much for hotel security.

"How long has it been since you called the police?"

"I didn't call the police. I haven't told anyone. Just you."

"What?" Ophelia's feet nearly stumbled as she ran across the parking lot to her car. Gabrielle had been kidnapped and Jared hadn't even called police? "You have to call 911.

Right away. Report it as a kidnapping and tell them you think he might hurt her. I'll be there soon and I'm going to call Kyle, too."

"No!" Jared's voice rose through the phone. "Wait! No police! If we call the cops or involve law enforcement in any way, he'll kill her."

"It's normal to think that way." Ophelia reached her car and yanked her keys from her bag. "But that doesn't mean it's true."

"He left a note!"

Ophelia paused. Her car keys shook in her hand.

"Bobby left a note?" she repeated. Hope rose in her chest. "Jared, that means there is physical evidence we can track. Handwriting, fingerprints, maybe even DNA."

"It won't help!" Jared sounded desperate. "He made her write it!"

"Bobby made Gabrielle write the note herself?"

"Yeah," Jared said.

The fleeting hope she'd just begun to feel popped like a balloon.

"Okay," she said, "that's not ideal. But maybe we can still use it. Who knows what evidence we might find."

"I Said You Can't Involve the Police!" Jared shouted. "If you've ever cared about me, please just trust me on this!"

No. Ophelia rocked back on her heels. As much as she loved her cousin, she wasn't about to let him make the call on whether or not police should be involved. But she knew someone whom she did trust.

"I'm getting into my car now and switching my phone to hands-free," she said. "I need to put you on hold and there might be some weird clicks, but I promise I'm not going anywhere and I'll be back in a second."

She put him on hold, leaped into her car and dialed Kyle.

"Hello?" Kyle's warm and reassuring voice filled the line. "Isla was just filling me in on what you guys did and didn't find. Sounds like we might be dealing with a copycat, and Nolan said everyone's been gossiping about the RMK."

"Jared says that Bobby kidnapped Gabrielle and we can't go to the police or he'll kill her," she said quickly. "I'm on the phone with him now. I need your help and for you to hear what's going on. So I'm going to mute you and then put you on the call with him via three-way." Which was risky, but she hoped Jared was too distracted to see the new name popping up on the screen. "You'll be able to hear us, but we won't be able to hear you. Okay?"

She'd just thrown a lot of information at Kyle quickly and hoped he'd been able to process it all.

"Okay," he said, and it was amazing just how much strength and security moved through her at hearing him speak just that one word. "Where are you now?"

"In my car." She peeled out of the parking lot and onto the road.

"Where are you headed?"

"To come get you." She hadn't even realized that was what she was planning on doing until the words left her lips. "So that we can go to the hotel and see Jared. I know he doesn't want police involved, but I can't do this without you."

"And you don't have to."

She glanced at the clock. Jared had been on hold for less than thirty seconds, but she imagined to him it felt like an eternity. She muted Kyle and then added Jared to the call.

"Hey, Jared," she said. "I'm back. I'm in my car and heading to the hotel."

"You can't come here," he said. His breathing was coming even faster and shallower now, like he was gasping for air. "Or he'll kill her!"

"Take a deep breath," she said, trying to think of the information Kyle would need to put the right wheels in motion to find Gabrielle. "We're going to find Gabrielle and we're going to help her. But to do that I need you to focus. How long has it been since you've seen her?"

There was a pause on the line for moment, and she worried he'd either hung up or passed out.

"An hour," he said finally. "Maybe an hour and a half."

"And you said the last place you saw her was her hotel room?"

"Yeah," Jared said. "She was really upset and said I never should've involved you in our business. She wanted to be alone. When I went to check on her she was gone. But her stuff was all still here and she'd left a note saying she was with Bobby."

"You said it was in Gabrielle's handwriting. Can you read it to me?"

There was another pause and then the rustle of papers.

"'Dear Jared,'" he began to read. "'I am so very sorry to do this to you on our wedding day. But I've realized that Bobby is the love of my life. He and I are meant to be together forever where the mountains meet the sky.

"'If you love me please forget about me. Bobby has promised to give me a good life. But if you call the police, bring law enforcement in or try to find me, then he will kill both me and himself, so that we can be together forever.

"'If you love me, don't tell anyone I've gone to be with Bobby, because you'll be putting my life in danger. I will love you forever but I have to go be with Bobby now.

"'Gabrielle.'"

Ophelia sucked in a breath, hoping that Kyle had caught every word and also wondering if that was what people sounded like when they were writing a goodbye letter to their fiancé with a gun to their head.

"That expression 'where the mountains meet the sky' means something right?" she said. "Isn't that what you called the land her parents bought for you guys to build your house?"

Jared didn't answer. It sounded like he was talking to someone else in the room.

"Jared?" Ophelia asked. "You there?"

"Sorry, I'm talking to Grandma Evelyn about the flowers. I've got to call you back."

The call went dead. She called back and Jared didn't answer. But she could see Kyle's house ahead now. His strong form was standing by the end of his driveway, with Rocky alert at his side. There were no vehicles in the driveway. Looked like Alice was out and he hadn't managed to replace his truck yet.

Kyle pocketed his phone as she drove up.

"I've alerted both Patricia at the Santa Fe PD and Chase at MCK9 of the situation," he said as he and Rocky jogged over, "including the facts that the kidnapper threatened to kill Gabrielle if police are involved, her fiancé is currently refusing to cooperate with law enforcement and that we need to search for her under the radar. But law enforcement will be on the lookout for anyone trying to take her out of the country either through the airports and over the border. Good news is that Meadow has arrived and is going to be taking Alice and Brody to a safe house."

"Got it," she said. "Get in. I think I might know where Gabrielle is. But I don't know for sure."

He opened the back door for Rocky. The K-9 leaped in. Then Kyle got in the passenger side.

"Where the mountains meet the sky," he said. "You know where that is?"

"I think so." Ophelia's hands clenched the steering wheel tightly. "That's the exact phrase they used to describe this plot of land near Pecos Wilderness that her parents bought for them to build a house. I went up there a few weeks ago to help Jared tie balloons to the trees for him to surprise her with, when he took her up there to show her. So, that has to be a clue? The solution to finding her couldn't be that simple, could it?"

Kyle's eyes flickered to the bright blue sky above, and he seemed to be praying. Then he asked, "How about you start driving that direction and we'll sort it out as we go."

"Okay." She pulled out of the driveway and started toward the highway that led to the Pecos Wilderness.

"So you think Gabrielle left Jared a clue to where Bobby was taking her?" Kyle asked.

"I think so," she said. "But I can't be sure." For all she knew they were driving in the completely wrong direction. "If it is a clue, then Gabrielle clearly planted it for Jared and he missed it."

"Well, he seemed incredibly distraught," Kyle said. "Maybe he's so upset he can't see the obvious. People miss all kinds of things when they're upset. But something about this theory doesn't sit right with you?"

"It's too simple," Ophelia admitted. "And in my experience most things are more complicated than that."

"It would also mean that Bobby missed the fact that

she put it in there," Kyle said. "Or maybe Bobby got her to use that phrase to lure Jared there, either to kill Jared or to kill Gabrielle somewhere her fiancé is certain to find her."

"So we could be driving into a trap," Ophelia said. "Or it could be nothing. I could be completely wrong. What if we get there and she's not there? What if it turns out I just wasted your time on a hunch and it's nothing but a wild-goose chase that keeps us from finding her?"

Kyle reached out his hand into the empty space between them. She took it and let the comforting warmth and strength of his fingers envelop hers.

"I don't know if Bobby is serious in his threats to kill Gabrielle," Kyle admitted. "But if Bobby really did kill both John Doe and Chloe, then it's very possible he will, especially if he thinks he's losing control of the situation. I also don't know if he has any way of knowing if police are involved or not, or if that's just a bluff. Maybe Gabrielle is right in thinking Bobby was well connected inside the police. But remember, it's my job to glean all the information I can and follow it until it leads me to the answers I need. Okay? You tell me the information you've got and I'll make the call. That's what we do."

Yeah, it was. And she had to trust they were both excellent at what they did.

"Okay." Slowly, she pulled her hand from his and then both of her hands through her hair. "Two months ago, Jared took me to see a plot of land that Gabrielle's parents were buying for them. He was making the down payment, and they were going to pay him back."

"Do you think you'd be able to find it?" Kyle asked.

"I'm pretty sure," she said. "I've got a good memory for details."

"Okay, we drive up there in your car," Kyle said. "I'm going to get in the back with Rocky and stay low, so if anybody's watching they will think you're driving up there alone. When we get there, Rocky and I will take a look around. If there's any signs of recent activity out there, we call for backup."

She pulled into the right-hand lane and slowed as he unbuckled his seat belt and climbed into the back seat beside his partner. They left the city and started toward the Rockies. She gritted her teeth.

"As much as I trust your memory," Kyle said. "I'm also going to call Isla and see if she can check property records to get an exact address for us. The property has to be in either Jared or Gabrielle's name."

He dialed and a moment later she heard Isla answer. But Ophelia tuned out his call and fixed her eyes on the road ahead, watching each intersection as they drove deeper and deeper into the untamed wilderness and counting on her memory to steer them right and lead them in the right direction.

She was sure she turned here. And there? No, wait. It had actually been two roads ahead over on her right.

Kyle ended the call and leaned forward between the seats. His brow creased with worry lines.

"The good news is that Isla thinks she's identified the jewelry store that sold the cuff links as one in Las Vegas," he said. "The bad news is she can't find any records for a Jared Clarke or Gabrielle Martinez owning a property anywhere near the Pecos Wilderness or even in the Santa Fe area."

The words hit her like a punch in the gut.

Had she remembered it wrong? Was she just driving deeper and deeper into the Rockies chasing a faulty memory?

"Maybe I was wrong, and it was registered under her parents or my great-aunt Evelyn?"

"I asked her to check by last name," he said. "Nothing under Evelyn Clarke, and while Martinez is a very common last name, there've been no new sales under that name the past six months."

She didn't even know what that meant.

But before she could worry about it, she saw a narrow road coming up ahead on her right. It was unmarked, but she could see the remnants of the ribbons where she'd once strung balloons hanging tattered from the trees and bleached from the sun.

"Well, I don't know who owns it," she said. "But we're here now."

"Okay." Kyle's voice came from the back seat. "Go slow. Keep an eye out and be prepared to get out of here in a moment's notice."

"Understood." She turned down the narrow dirt path.

"Lord," she prayed, "keep me safe and help me see what I need to see."

"Amen," Kyle echoed.

The cabin appeared in the woods through the trees ahead. It was wooden and faded, barely more than a shack. The dilapidated building had also been the only structure on it the last time she'd been there and now it looked even smaller than before. Then she saw the white van parked beyond it.

"Okay, we've got more than what we need," Kyle said. "Let's get out of here—"

But then a desperate and panicked cry rose on the air, freezing the words on Kyle's tongue and cutting a chill through Ophelia's heart like a knife.

"Help me!" Gabrielle screamed from somewhere within the shack. "Somebody help me! Please!"

"Ophelia, call 911!" Kyle shouted, leaping from the back seat and summoning Rocky to his side. "If something kicks off I want you to drive out of here and whatever happens don't get out of the car!"

He'd already slammed the door and started running toward the cabin with his gun drawn when he heard Ophelia call his name.

"Kyle! Stop! It might be a trap! You might be running into danger."

"I know." He stopped and looked back. "But that's the job I signed up for."

He was a law enforcement officer who'd sworn an oath to rescue and protect those in trouble. Even when his life was on the line or it meant running into danger. Somewhere inside that shack Gabrielle was calling for help. He had no choice but to do whatever it took to rescue her.

"But you could get killed," Ophelia pleaded.

Yeah, he knew that, too, and yet the depth of worry in her eyes was so strong it took all the power he had to break her gaze.

"You're right," he said. "But I'm going to stand up, do what I know is right, and trust God to keep us safe and make it all right in the end."

She nodded and pulled her phone from her bag. Together, Kyle and Rocky turned and ran swiftly toward the cabin, staying close to the tree line and away from any sightlines that might put him in the line of fire.

Two voices rose on the wind.

One was male and his bellowing voice was punctuated

with curses and shaking with rage. "Shut up! Just shut your face now! Not one more word out of you. I'm done putting up with your nonsense!"

The other was Gabrielle's, bargaining one moment, screaming and crying the next, as if desperately trying to figure out what to say to calm down the monster holding her captive. "It's not what you think. Jared and I are really in love—"

He snorted. "You're a liar!"

"What do you want from me?" Gabrielle shouted. "You want money? I'll get you money! I promise. Just let me go!"

"You think I'm letting you out of my sight? You so much as flinch and I'll kill you."

Kyle glanced through the filthy window at the scene unfolding in front of him. Gabrielle was down on her knees, tears rolling down her cheek. Her hands were unbound and yet an ugly bruise under her eye made it clear her kidnapper wouldn't hesitate to strike. The man he guessed was Bobby stood over her, limping from a left leg injury Kyle recognized all too well, as he paced back and forth waving a gun in her face. And for the first time, Kyle got a really good look at the masked man who'd shot at them in the barn, tried to kidnap Ophelia and probably killed Chloe. He was in his late twenties or even early thirties, with unremarkable brown hair and narrow eyes, and one pupil so pale that Kyle wondered if he was blind in one eye.

So this was Bobby? Kyle had never seen his face before.

Rocky growled softly, and even without looking down, Kyle could sense his partner's hackles rise. His partner could detect the smell of death. Kyle thought of Chloe's locket, which had been snapped in half. Maybe Bobby had kept some kind of gruesome trophies of his kills nearby.

"You're not thinking right," Gabrielle said. "Please just calm down and listen."

"I'm done listening to you!" He lunged toward her and aimed the gun between her eyes. "No more stories. No more lies. This time I'm in charge!"

Not if Kyle had anything to do about it. He raised his weapon, prayed that God would guide his hand and fired through the window, sending glass shattering across the floor. The bullet clipped the man in the shoulder before his finger could even brush the trigger.

He swore in pain. The gun fell from his hand and clattered to the ground. Then he pelted from the cabin and took off running down the mountain.

"Who's there?" Gabrielle called. "Jared?"

But Kyle didn't stop to answer her. He wasn't about to let her attacker escape.

He ran through the woods after the man who had to be Bobby.

"Agent Kyle West of the Mountain Country K-9 Unit!" his voice rose. His partner barked. "Stop! You're under arrest!"

The man was limping and bleeding, and yet dodging around trees and tumbling over rocks as he practically threw his body down the steep mountainside in a desperate attempt to get away.

Not this time.

Kyle leaped, catching the man by this unwounded shoulder and pulling him down to the ground. For moment they rolled and tumbled down the rocky mountainside, while Rocky ran after them. But it was Kyle who found his footing first.

"Stay down!" he shouted, standing over the wounded

man lying at his feet. "You put up an impressive fight. But Bobby Whatever-your-last-name-is, you're now under arrest for kidnapping and murder."

The sound of sirens filled the woods above him. Kyle read the man his rights. When he was done, the man swore. "I'm not Bobby, you idiot."

"Well, whoever you are, I'm arresting you." He hauled the man to his feet and cuffed his hands in front of him as gently as he could, so as to not aggravate his injury. Then he patted him down and found a wallet in his jacket pocket. He pulled out the driver's license. It was from Las Vegas. The photo matched. He read the name. "Dylan Brown. Is that your name?"

"Yeah!" Dylan shouted. "Told you I'm not Bobby! He was a stupid fool who didn't know when to quit!"

Whatever that meant.

"Is Bobby the man you killed in the barn?"

"I didn't kill anyone." Dylan scowled, his single, very pale iris gave his face an unsettlingly uneven look, and Kyle realized that must be why the mask he'd worn to commit his crimes had included a dark mesh that covered his eyes.

"Why did you kidnap Gabrielle?" Kyle demanded. "Why did you attack Ophelia?"

"Because I got tired of being used and treated like a fool. And that's all I'm going to say!"

Kyle looked down at Rocky. *I don't have a clue what to make of any of that. I'm just glad I finally got cuffs on this guy.* His partner growled softly. Did Dylan smell of a fresh death or had Kyle's hunch about trophies been right?

Voices rose from the trees. Backup had arrived. Kyle quickly snapped a photo of the man's face and driver's license and sent them off to Isla with the request she find out whatever she could about him. Then he turned and marched Dylan up the hill as he swore and complained.

Santa Fe PD officers and paramedics met him as he neared the top of the slope.

"This is Dylan Brown from Las Vegas," Kyle said. "He's under arrest for murder and kidnapping. He needs immediate medical attention, for a fresh bullet wound in the shoulder and another in the calf yesterday, which I'm guessing he didn't get medical treatment for. Don't underestimate him. He's tough."

"And I don't need a doctor," Dylan grumbled.

Kyle had no doubt that when they scratched the surface of this man's life they'd find a rough upbringing and very long criminal history.

Suddenly his mind flashed back to the RMK. The Rocky Mountain Killer had murdered three men ten years ago, then another three in the past few months. And like Dylan, Kyle thought there had to some be something tragic behind his cruelty.

Lord, what pain in the RMK's life led him to become the vindictive and taunting killer he is today? Help the MCK9 find him, and please heal the hearts of all those impacted by his crimes.

"Kyle!" Ophelia called. He looked up to see her running toward him. He jogged toward her. Instinctively his arms opened to embrace her. But instead, she stopped a few paces away from him and folded her arms across her chest, and he found himself doing the same.

"Gabrielle just left in an ambulance," she said. "Patricia Gonzales went with her. Gabrielle says that Bobby didn't hurt her beyond slapping and scaring her, and she was just in a hurry to get back to Jared. But she's promised to give

Patricia a full and complete statement." She smiled. "I'm so happy and relieved you finally got him."

Kyle frowned.

"Me, too," he said and thanked God for the fact. "But he says his name is not Bobby and he's carrying a Las Vegas driver's license that says he's Dylan Brown."

Ophelia blinked.

"Do you think he lied to Gabrielle about his name being Bobby?" she asked. "Or lied to you about his name being Dylan? Is it possible his ID is fake?"

"No idea," Kyle said. "But he clearly has some kind of history with her and he hates her. Did you notice he had two different colored eyes?"

"Yeah, it's called heterochromia," Ophelia said. "It's very rare in human DNA, impacting less than one percent of the population. It's much more common in animals. It could be heredity or the result of something he was exposed to as a young child."

"My impression is that this criminal hasn't had an easy life," Kyle said, "not that it justifies anything he's done. Thankfully, at this point, putting the case together becomes the prosecutor's job. I'm just glad we caught this guy, he's off the streets, this part of the case is over and I don't have to worry about my little guy and mother having to go stay in a safe house."

But even as he said the words a doubt crossed his mind. What if Dylan hadn't been working alone? Did he have an accomplice? Was it Bobby?

"And I can finally get back to my lab," Ophelia said. "Although I expect that I'm still going to have a wedding to show up at tonight. I don't think anything's going to stop those two from getting married, even if it's a five-minute ceremony."

And if they did, Kyle wouldn't be there. The guy had been caught. He wasn't her pretend wedding date anymore. Rocky barked softly and sniffed the air. Whatever the K-9 was alerting to, it wasn't Dylan.

"Sorry, he's been alerting since we got here," Kyle said. "Even though he's trained to detect bodies, sometimes cadaver dogs will detect something that's touched a corpse, like what was used to transport it recently."

"Well, you should go see what he wants to show you," Ophelia said.

Yeah, he should. And even though he'd finally caught his man, he hoped that whatever Rocky was signaling to would be that final piece of the puzzle that wrapped up the case for good. He turned to Rocky. "Show me."

Rocky barked and started sniffing the ground. The dog took off toward the cabin, which was now swarming with investigators. Kyle followed closely behind. The K-9 led him past the cabin, to a soft mound of earth and rock. The footsteps that surrounded it looked fresh. Rocky woofed confidently and sat in front of it.

"Good job," Kyle said sadly.

He crouched down and pulled the rocks back. It was the body of a young man. This time, the victim's body wasn't wrapped in anything, but just lay there in the shallow grave, under a pile of rocks. He heard Ophelia gasp and looked up to see her standing behind him.

"I thought we were done," she said. "You caught him. He's in custody where he won't be able to kill ever again."

"I know," Kyle said. Slowly he moved the rocks one by

one. “But I guess he managed to kill one more time before we could stop him.”

He sat back on his heels. Sadness filled his core as the face came into view.

It was Nolan.

ELEVEN

"We have three dead bodies." Kyle slapped the pictures of Chloe, John Doe and Nolan down on the interrogation table in front of Dylan. "Why these three? What do they have in common?"

It had been almost two hours since Rocky had led Kyle to Nolan's body. Nolan, like John Doe and Chloe before him, had taken a single gunshot wound to the chest. The time after that had passed in a blur as he coordinated with the police, crime scene techs and paramedics who'd retrieved the body and documented how it had been found. Once again, Ophelia had slipped off and headed back to town while he was busy doing his job and managing the scene. This time he'd caught her wave goodbye. But there'd been no time alone for a conversation, let alone a hug goodbye.

For all he knew, they'd never be alone like that again.

He'd returned to the same Santa Fe PD station where he'd interviewed Nolan just a few hours earlier. And since then, he'd been sitting in an interrogation room across from Dylan, locked in the same frustrating conversation as it went around in circles.

"I'm not telling you nothing!" Dylan said. Thankfully, both of his injuries had been minor and easy for paramedics to patch up.

Kyle looked down at Nolan's picture. The same man had sat in that very room a few hours earlier, after warning Kyle that someone had placed an explosive in his SUV. Not only had Dylan's fingerprints confirmed his identity, they'd also been found, along with explosive residue, on a bag found where Kyle's vehicle had been parked when the bomb had been planted, confirming Dylan was indeed the man Nolan had seen.

Nolan might've saved Kyle's life. But Kyle had been unable to save his.

"My colleague emailed me your rap sheet," Kyle said and opened the email from Isla on his phone. "You're right, you're Dylan Brown. No known aliases. And you've got a long record for theft, burglary and assault. But no murder, until these three. I'll ask you again, why them?"

Dylan crossed his arms leaned back in the chair. "I'm not a killer."

"Look, you're a muscle for hire," Kyle said. "You do jobs and favors for people. So, my theory is someone asked you to murder these three people, tamper with the gas tank of my vehicle and terrorize both Gabrielle Martinez and Ophelia Clarke. I think that if I hadn't stopped you, you would've killed both Gabrielle and Ophelia. Why? Who has a vendetta against all these people?"

Dylan cursed under his breath and didn't answer.

Lord, how can I be so close to getting an answer and still have nothing?

There was a knock on the door. Rocky's head rose. The K-9's tail started to thump on the floor, letting Kyle know that whoever was on the other side of the door was a friend.

Kyle stood. "I'll give you a moment to think."

Dylan only grunted in response. Kyle and Rocky stepped

out into the hallway, where he found Meadow and her K-9 partner, Grace, waiting for him.

"I hear congratulations are in order," she said. "I was told you got your man."

Kyle glanced back through the small, reinforced window at where Dylan still sat at the table. "I know I should feel more relieved. I am certain he's the man behind every violent crime related to this case and yet I'd just feel better if I knew what his motive was."

"And you don't think it's related to the RMK?" Meadow asked.

"No." Kyle shook his head. He knew he should be relieved that the criminal he'd been chasing was finally off the street. But still it felt like something was missing. He quickly ran Meadow through all of the details of the case as he knew them so far, starting with the moment Ophelia heard gunshots.

"What if Dylan is in love with Gabrielle?" Meadow asked. "Wasn't that your original theory? So it turns out his name is Dylan and not Bobby, but it could be that simple. He came to the wedding looking to kill Jared but shot John Doe by mistake. He killed Chloe for trying to warn Ophelia that he was coming to stop the wedding and attacked you and Ophelia for trying to investigate the case. Finally, he killed Nolan in revenge for telling you about the fact that he tampered with the SUV. It all fits."

"It's too simple." Ophelia's words from earlier brushed the back of my mind. *"And in my experience most things are more complicated than that."*

"Except who's Bobby?" Kyle said, "And why did an unidentified blond man who looked like the groom get lured to the barn where the reception was taking place on the day before the wedding?"

It was like a sweater that only looked neat and tidy until someone pulled on one the loose threads and then the whole thing unraveled.

"I don't know," Meadow admitted. "By the way, I ran into Ophelia in the waiting room. She was just dropping by on the way to the wedding, and she asked me to give you this."

She picked up something soft and white off a chair and handed it to him. It was his short-sleeved shirt that Ophelia had borrowed. Without even thinking, he held it close to his face and smelled in the scent of her.

The fact that she'd chosen to drop it off at the police station where he was working instead of his home told him everything he needed to know—their time working closely together was well and truly over. They wouldn't be going for long nighttime walks or sharing coffee together in the morning. There'd never again be a reason for them to suddenly throw their arms around each other, or for their lips to unexpectedly meet in a kiss. And that was how he wanted it, right? Because he'd decided he wasn't looking for a relationship and obviously neither was she.

Meadow looked at him curiously and he wondered if she'd caught him cradling the shirt.

"I found out why your mother has been going to the pharmacy so often," she said. "Turns out she has a crush on the pharmacist. I met him earlier today when we popped in to buy a few overnight things, when we were still thinking that we'd have to go to the safe house. He's a nice guy. He's a widower her age, and a man of faith. I think she wants to date him but is worried about how you'll react."

"That's ridiculous." Kyle crossed his arms.

"Is it?" Meadow said. "Sorry if this is too personal, but your mom also mentioned that your father was bad news. She told me about the whole dating site debacle, and my impression was that she thought that maybe if you started dating you'd be okay with her starting a new relationship, too."

Really? Was his mother holding herself back because of him?

"I don't have a problem with my mom starting a new life," Kyle said. "I'm not going to start dating, because I'm worried for Brody and need to focus on being his father. I can't risk starting a relationship that might fail or getting Brody attached to someone who might leave our lives. What if I fall in love and marry someone, and then it doesn't work out?"

And what about his own heart? All this time Kyle had kept telling himself he was choosing to be single for fear of hurting Brody or putting him through the turmoil that Kyle had grown up in. But the way his heart beat painfully even now at the memory of just how terrified he'd been when Ophelia was in danger made him realize that maybe Brody wasn't the only who he was trying to save from pain.

"I guess that's a choice you need to make," Meadow said. "I had to walk away from someone I loved once. I didn't have a choice and it broke my heart." She glanced down at the shirt Kyle was still holding in his hands. "Look, I only just met Ophelia today and already it's clear to me how much you two care about each other. And that's rare. So you're just going to have to decide if that's a risk you're willing to take."

The sun dipped low in the New Mexico sky, sending pink and gold streaks across the horizon. As Ophelia walked down the path to Cherish Ranch's outdoor wedding chapel, dark purple shadows spread out beneath her feet. Truth was, she wasn't sure what to think about the fact that Jared and Gabrielle were still getting married, although with a much smaller celebration than originally planned.

Then again, if she had the opportunity to marry a man whom she loved with her whole heart, would she let anything stand in her way?

The outdoor chapel itself was simple and beautiful, with rows of chairs overlooking the glorious vista and a simple archway of wooden branches stretching up to the sky.

She sat in the back row, in her favorite turquoise dress and sandals. Ophelia couldn't remember ever seeing a more romantic scene or feeling such a depth of sadness inside her own heart. She closed her eyes and tried to settle her thoughts, only to find Kyle's handsome face fill her mind.

Lord, I've never liked a man as much as I like Kyle. He's not just handsome, funny, kind and brave. He likes the things about me that I like about myself. I want a man like him by my side. And yet, I looked him in the eyes and told him I could never let it happen. Have I been so convinced that Your plan for me doesn't include that kind of happiness that I closed my heart?

"Oh, I'm so glad you're here, dear," Great-Aunt Evelyn's voice cut through her prayers. Ophelia opened her eyes as her aunt slid into the chair beside her, in a resplendent yellow dress that somehow reminded her of baby ducks without looking the slightest bit cutesy.

"I think you're meant to sit in the front row," Ophelia said.

"I know, I just wanted to sit with you." Evelyn's delicate hand patted Ophelia's affectionately, and Ophelia realized for the first time just how frail her great-aunt had gotten. "This whole wedding thing doesn't feel right and it never really has. You know I don't like being negative and I promised my grandson I wouldn't question his decisions, but maybe I was wrong to support this wedding. What do you think?"

She fixed her eyes on Ophelia's face. They were the same shade of blue as hers. And Ophelia realized this might actually be the first time her great-aunt had asked her opinion about something significant.

"I think Jared really loves Gabrielle and will stop at nothing to marry her," Ophelia said.

"I can understand loving someone so much you want to marry them immediately," Evelyn said, "even in the face of tragedy. I remember when I was a little girl hearing stories about people lining up at the church to get married days before their fella shipped off to the war. My mama said when you loved somebody you don't let the bad things in life stop you from the good ones."

Maybe like eating scrambled eggs in the morning, Ophelia thought, and playing trucks with Brody in the sandbox.

"I never had a wedding," Evelyn added, almost wistfully. "I always wanted one, but we didn't have the money. The business was struggling and it was either pay the rent or get married. So we just eloped one night and then my mom made us chicken dinner. I didn't even have a dress."

Ophelia's eyes widened. "But what about all those beautiful wedding pictures you have up on the wall?"

"Oh, we just took those in the park behind the church three years later, because we'd never gotten pictures and we'd been given this beautiful set of frames. I was actually four months' pregnant with Jared's dad by then. I just hid the little bump behind my bouquet."

"You never told me any of that," Ophelia said.

Ophelia searched her seventy-four-year-old great-aunt's face and realized that she'd never heard a story about a time they hadn't been well off.

"That sounds really lovely," Ophelia said. "I thought if I ever got married you'd be disappointed if I didn't do a big wedding like Jared."

"Oh, you do what's right for you." Evelyn patted her hand. "It's not for me to tell you what to do. Or judge. I just give you my best advice and leave it up to you."

Ophelia hid a smile. She couldn't imagine her great-aunt was about to start keeping her opinions to herself, especially if Ophelia ever did end up having the unexpected blessing of finding a man to marry her. But it was kind of nice to know that was the kind of person Evelyn wanted to be.

"I mean, I did my best to keep my mouth shut about this whole wedding mess and keep writing checks every time Jared said he needed me to." Evelyn waved her hands in the air. "But now I'm beginning to think I should've pushed back instead of just going ahead and paying for all this."

"What do you mean you paid for all this?" Ophelia asked. "You paid for the wedding? I thought the bride's family pays for the wedding. Or the couple themselves."

And wasn't Gabrielle's family supposed to be unbelievably wealthy?

"Oh, there as some problem with the international payments," Evelyn said, "and they said they were going to go to my bank with me and sort it all out when they got here." But then Gabrielle's parents had never showed up. Ophelia thought back to how stressed her great-aunt had been about everything when she'd asked Ophelia to step in as a bridesmaid. "Jared just kept calling me up and saying that Gabrielle was upset, and they needed money for this and money for that. The wedding venue. Dresses. Catering. A private jet to whisk them off to Mexico for their honeymoon. I don't even know where it all went."

Ophelia's mouth went dry.

"Auntie." Ophelia gently reached for Evelyn's and took it in both of hers. "How much money have you given Jared and Gabrielle?"

"Oh, I don't know." Evelyn didn't meet her eyes and shrugged. "Jared would just give me these different bank accounts to wire money to. Gabrielle always said her parents would pay me back."

But Gabrielle's parents were conveniently overseas and had never materialized. For all she knew, Gabrielle had been lying about her parents the whole time and they never intended to pay Evelyn back a single cent. The taste in Ophelia's mouth turned bitter. "It was a lot of money, wasn't it? More than you could afford to give."

Now she could actually see tears building in the corner of her great-aunt's eyes. Ophelia's heart ached. She enveloped her great-aunt in her arms and hugged her.

"You know I love you, right?" Ophelia asked. "I know we don't always agree on everything. And we don't always like the words each other says. But I love you, you matter to me, and I'm sorry that Jared and Gabrielle were taking advantage of you."

For a long moment her great-aunt hugged her back and didn't say anything. Then she pulled away and stood.

"I'm fine." Evelyn patted Ophelia on the shoulder. "You are sweet and I am so thankful to have a great-niece like you. Now I'm just going to go check in and see what's keeping Jared and Gabrielle so long. They left the hotel before I did and I can't believe they haven't arrived yet."

Evelyn started down the path toward the main lodge. The toes of Ophelia's sandals tapped against the ground as she fought the urge to rush to the lodge, look for Jared herself and ask him how he could possibly be so selfish as to take advantage of his grandmother like that. She had half a mind to take her great-aunt to the bank and see what she could do to help her get her money back. Not to mention asking the ranch for receipts to see just how much of her money really went to the wedding.

Without even pausing to think about why, she pulled out her phone and called Kyle.

The phone rang twice, then clicked.

"Hey, Kyle, it's Ophelia. I don't know if this has anything to do with anything but I just found out that Gabrielle and Jared have been taking advantage of my great-aunt and getting her to pay for everything—"

"Hello, you've reached Agent Kyle West of the Mountain Country K-9 Task Force." His voice came down the line crisp, professional and slightly tinny. "Please leave your message at the tone."

She hung up. What had she been thinking? The masked man had been arrested. The case was over. She couldn't just call Kyle on a whim anymore to offload about what her family was doing and how she felt about it. Somehow in just twenty-four hours they'd gone from being colleagues who'd barely spoken, to a professional pair that worked together, to friends, and then what? To something else entirely that she didn't yet have the courage to try to put into words.

It was only then that she noticed a red dot on the corner of the screen telling her that she'd missed a call. She clicked on it hoping it was Kyle.

It was Isla.

Ophelia looked around. It didn't look like the wedding was about to start anytime soon. She stood up, walked down the path toward the parking lot and dialed Isla's number. She answered before it had even rung once. "Hey, Ophelia! Aren't you supposed to be at a wedding right now?"

"I am, but the bride and groom are running late," she said. "I missed a call from you?"

"You did!" She could hear Isla smiling down the phone. "I tracked down the cuff link to the jewelry store where it was bought and I think I found our John Doe."

"Really?" Now, that was good news. "Who is he?"

"Robert Wesley Norrs, professional gambler and online investor, last seen in Las Vegas a week ago," Isla said. "And yes, I was able to get a visual match to our John Doe from the jewelry store surveillance cameras."

"Robert as in Bobby," Ophelia said.

"I've got a picture," Isla said. "Want me to send it through?"

"Absolutely." A second later her phone dinged and Ophelia looked down to see a handsome blond man with arrogant eyes. "That's our John Doe. He's the man who was shot in the barn yesterday. Have you shown this to Kyle yet?"

"I left a message on his phone," Isla said, "but he didn't call me back. But get this, last year Robert came into the Las Vegas jewelry store with his fiancée, Lisette Austin. He bought her a huge diamond ring as well as the pair of cuff links for him. She said it was to celebrate their engagement. From what I could glean from his social media, Lisette dumped Robert and left town after a gambling loss."

"Who's Lisette Austin, though?" Ophelia said. "I've never heard of her."

"That's because she doesn't exist," Isla said. "At least not under that name. A woman matching her description is suspected of romancing and even marrying men under fake identities and robbing them blind in Connecticut, Texas, Florida and Vermont. Sometimes she's even suspected of killing them. But they've never managed to track down who she really is or pin down her identity. It's all conjecture. No proof."

Ophelia's phone pinged. Then a black-and-white picture appeared on the screen of a woman with long blond hair. Ophelia's mouth gaped. Despite the different hair color, the face was clear. "That's my cousin's fiancée, Gabrielle."

Isla gasped. "Are you sure?"

"Definitely." And now she was pretty certain wherever Jared and "Gabrielle" were now, they weren't about to show up here to get married. No wonder "Gabrielle" hadn't wanted police poking around and had been in such a hurry to marry Jared.

"According to the files I can read on her, she's a pretty talented manipulator," Isla said. "She zeroes in on wealthy and lonely men, convinces them that she's in love with them and then bleeds them dry. Sometimes she even cons their family members out of money."

Like Evelyn. Ophelia thought back to all their interactions with Gabrielle in the past twenty-four hours. The way Gabrielle would cling to Ophelia like they were best buddies, or smile one moment and cry theatrically. "It was like she was always trying to figure out what button to push to make me like her and could never quite find the right one. How many ex-husbands is she suspected of killing?"

"Four," Isla said. "Plus, quite a few she just robbed."

"Then either way my cousin is in trouble," Ophelia said.

"Again, I've got to stress that police have never successfully pegged anything on this woman," Isla said. "There's not even a single warrant out anywhere for her arrest. She's too slippery to be charged with anything, and all we have are theories."

And Ophelia didn't peddle in theories. Only facts. And the fact was there wasn't a single scrap of DNA, fingerprint evidence or anything else sitting back at the forensic laboratory that pointed to Gabrielle committing a crime, let alone killing anyone.

Lord, please help me find the facts I need to protect my cousin and stop her from hurting anyone else.

"My great-aunt said they were taking a private jet to Mexico for their honeymoon," she said. "If they disappear into Mexico, there's any number of ways she could kill my cousin and vanish."

She heard the sound of Isla typing quickly. Ophelia could feel all the evidence she'd gathered in the past twenty-four hours finally clicking together in her mind.

So Gabrielle was a con artist who romanced men for their money. She got engaged to Robert Willian Norrs, aka RWN, aka Bobby. Then she moved on to Jared. But then Bobby wasn't about to let her go so easily. He started stalking her and came to Santa Fe to stop the wedding. And then what? Bobby was murdered. How did she prove Gabrielle had anything to do with Bobby's, Chloe's and Nolan's deaths?

Bobby could've exposed Gabrielle as a con artist. Chloe had talked to Bobby and tried to share her concerns with Ophelia. Nolan had given Gabrielle an alibi for the time of

Bobby's murder and then warned Kyle of the bomb Dylan had planted in his car.

So they were all liabilities. But it was still all circumstantial.

And how did Dylan fit into this? He definitely didn't fit the type Gabrielle would pursue romantically.

"Okay, I've found them," Isla said. "Gabrielle and Jared are at the Santa Fe Airport now, scheduled to fly to Tijuana. I'm going to alert officials not to let them on the plane. But they'll only be able to delay them. They won't be able to stop them from just walking out of the airport and vanishing."

"I'm heading there now," Ophelia said. She climbed into her car and plugged her phone into the vehicle's hands-free speaker. "Hopefully, they can delay Jared long enough for me to get there and try to talk to him. My cousin is so blindly in love he's not going to believe anything they tell him. But maybe if I can get him alone, I can talk some sense into him."

"Tell him he's not the first person she's fooled," Isla said.

"I don't think that's going to help," Ophelia said. The problem with being the kind of man who just arrogantly assumed everyone was going to do what he wanted was he wouldn't accept he'd been duped by a con woman. "I'm going to hang up and try Kyle again. In the meantime, send me everything you can on Gabrielle for now."

"Will do," Isla said. "Police still don't know her real identity, but there are a lot of photos of her with different hair and eye colors."

They ended the call and the technical analyst's final two words continued to ring in Ophelia's mind. *Eye color. Eye color.* What was her mind trying to tell her or remind her of?

Ophelia pulled out of the parking lot and drove down the twisting mountain road. The Santa Fe Airport was on the outskirts of town. If she stuck to back roads she could be there in fifteen minutes, give or take. She dialed Kyle's number. But again, it went through to voice mail. All right, so he must still be in interrogation.

Now what? Just how brave could she be? Just how certain was she that she was right? She gritted her teeth and dialed Detective Patricia Gonzales directly.

"Gonzales." The detective's voice was on the line in a moment.

"Hi, it's CSI Ophelia Clarke," she said. "I'm so sorry to do this, but I know Kyle West is in the police station right now and I have urgent information for the case and need to talk to him immediately."

"Understood," she said.

The phone went silent as Ophelia was put on hold. She drove and prayed. Then she heard a new call beginning to ring on her phone. It was Kyle.

Thank You, God.

She ended the call with Patricia and answered.

"Ophelia, hi!" Kyle sounded flustered. "Someone just knocked on the door of my interrogation room and said it was an emergency. I've been going around in circles with Dylan for hours. Whatever he's hiding, he's not about to crack."

"Isla has identified our John Doe as a gambler from Las Vegas called Robert Wesley Norrs," she said quickly. The sky was growing darker around her. "So that's our Bobby. He was engaged to marry Gabrielle, who at the time was going by the name Lisette. Gabrielle was there when he bought the cuff links to celebrate their engagement. Maybe he brought them to return to her—"

"Or maybe she demanded them back," Kyle said. She could practically hear the wheels in his head turning.

"Gabrielle is a con woman with a history of crossing the country, changing her name and look, romancing men and robbing them," Ophelia said. "She's even suspected of killing a few."

Kyle sucked a breath.

"Turns out she got Jared to milk my great-aunt for a whole lot of money," she went on. "She and Jared are supposed to hop a plane to Tijuana, and Isla's asked police to delay them."

She quickly outlined her theory from how Gabrielle had conned multiple men under various identities, set her sights on Jared in the hotel, convinced him to marry her and take advantage of Evelyn's generous nature to weasel her out of money. But then her last target, Bobby, hadn't wanted to give up on her easily and tracked her down. Maybe she'd even led him on romantically while being engaged to Jared, in order to con more money of out him. Bobby had said something to Chloe, which made Gabrielle's roommate a liability. Nolan was Gabrielle's alibi for the time of Bobby's murder.

Bobby, Chloe and Nolan had all been liabilities, who knew something about Gabrielle that could've thwarted her scheme.

She switched her headlights on as the last sliver of the sun vanished beyond the horizon.

"But I don't have evidence," she said, "and we need evidence. Otherwise, I won't be able to convince Jared not to trust her. He'll never believe me. Police have no reason to detain them indefinitely. And sooner or later he'll just take off with Gabrielle, she'll kill him and I'll never see him alive again."

She could hear Kyle praying quietly down the line. She joined in his prayers.

Lord, help me trust in the work I do and the skills I've honed that You've given me. I'm used to noticing the little things. Sometimes the smallest thing is the key to catching a serial killer.

"Gabrielle was only wearing one contact yesterday," Ophelia said suddenly. "What if she doesn't need them for her eyesight but only to disguise her eye color. And if she was only wearing one—"

"She might have the same DNA condition as Dylan," Kyle said.

"Heterochromia," Ophelia said. "Which means he might not only be her accomplice, but also her brother."

"Which might explain why he won't turn on her," Kyle said, "and also what I need to get him to crack." He whistled. "You're incredible, Ophelia? You know that?"

Then before she could reply she heard the sound of a door opening and closing again, a chair scraping and Kyle setting the phone down on the table, without ending the call.

"I'm still not talking," Dylan said.

"It doesn't matter if you talk or not," Kyle said. "Because we know that Gabrielle is your sister. She's been conning men into marrying her, robbing them and even killing a few. And I expect she's going to pin it all on you, cut a sweet little deal with prosecutors and tell them that you're the one who's been making her do it. Who do you think a jury's going to believe? Your sister or you?"

Silence crackled on the line. Ophelia held her breath and prayed that Kyle's bluff would work. She could see the airport in the distance now, the beautiful adobe orange rectangles and squares, looking like something built from children's blocks.

Lord, please help me get through to Jared. Protect my heart and mind.

"My sister's a liar!" Dylan's voice shouted down the phone. "Her name isn't even Gabrielle. It's Dorothy Brown. I had nothing to do with all her nonsense and scams. She just called me because she needed help with this Bobby person. She wanted me to meet him in the barn, rough him up a bit and convince him to leave her alone. But apparently she got there first, they started fighting and he threw a pair of cuff links at her. Anyway, she lost it. So, when I got there turns out she's already killed him and begs me to make it look like she didn't do it. I've been cleaning up her mess ever since. Take care of this person, take care of that or that person, I've had enough of her. Now get me a lawyer! I want to cut a deal!"

Prayers of thanksgiving filled Ophelia's heart. Now police had enough to arrest Gabrielle, or Dorothy or whatever her name was, and protect her from hurting Jared or anyone else ever again. It would still be a matter of whom a jury believed and a testimony wasn't the same as DNA evidence, but it was a good start and she was confident they'd get what they needed to put her away for good.

She heard Kyle stepping out of the interrogation room and informing someone that Dylan had requested a lawyer and that a warrant needed to be issued for Dorothy Brown aka Gabrielle Martinez.

The airport grew closer. A construction vehicle with reflective triangular stickers was parked at the side of the road. A woman with long blond and curly hair, reflective sunglasses and bright orange vest stepped in front of Ophelia's vehicle and held up a stop sign.

Ophelia slowed to a stop and rolled the window down.

"You gotta turn back!" The woman strode over to Ophelia's car. "We've got a downed power line ahead."

Ophelia glanced at the road ahead. She didn't see any downed power lines.

Then she felt something sharp jab into her side. A quick and painful blast of electricity shot through her limbs. She cried out in pain.

"Ophelia!" Kyle's voice yelled down the phone line and filled the car.

Ophelia whimpered from the lingering pain and she glanced in disbelief at the woman who'd just jabbed a stun gun into her side.

It was Gabrielle.

"Can you hear me, Agent West?" Gabrielle leaned into the car. Her voice was cold, calculating and stripped of all the fake sweetness that had once dripped from it like honey. "Nice try getting someone to delay my flight and separate me and Jared. You think I didn't know how to slip out a window? But now I have Ophelia and you tell Evelyn that if she ever wants to see her again, she's got twenty-four hours to wire me three million dollars. I'm getting out of this state, one way or another, and if I so much as see a police car or helicopter, Ophelia dies."

TWELVE

"Don't you hurt her!" Kyle shouted down the phone line, even as he heard Gabrielle ordering Ophelia to end the call and toss the phone. The phone clattered.

His stomach wrenched. Rocky whined as if sensing his fear.

"What's going on?" Meadow asked. He looked up to see the US marshal and Grace running down the hallway toward him. "Your voice reverberated all the way to the lobby."

"Ophelia's been kidnapped by a serial killer," he said. "It was the bride all along. She says if she even sees a cop car or helicopter, she'll kill her."

"Where are they?" Meadow asked.

"They just left the airport," he said. "I don't know where they're heading."

"Let's go," Meadow turned sharply and ran for the side door, her K-9 partner at her side. "Thankfully I flew in and my Jeep's a rental without any police marking. You can fill me in as we go." She tossed him her keys. "You drive, I don't know Santa Fe."

Seconds later they were in the vehicle speeding down the highway. Meadow was in the passenger seat and on the phone with dispatch, putting law enforcement across the state on the lookout for Gabrielle and Ophelia, and filling in the Santa Fe State Police's emergency response unit on the details of the kidnapping and ransom demands, so a crisis response officer could be in touch with Evelyn. Rocky and Grace sat at attention beside each other in the back seat. Kyle's fingers tightened on the steering wheel. He glanced to where he'd plugged his cell phone into the hands-free. The call still hadn't ended. By the sound of things, the phone was now hidden somewhere in Ophelia's back seat, live but on mute, like she'd let him listen in to her conversation with Jared hours before.

Minutes ticked past. The airport loomed ahead in the distance, but there was no sign of Ophelia's car anywhere. But if Ophelia had hoped to be able to give Kyle directions on where she was and how to find her, it wasn't working. Instead, tense silence spread down the line, punctuated only by cryptic directions from Gabrielle to Ophelia like "turn here," "there" and "stop fidgeting."

Help me, Lord, please give me the information I need to find her.

He focused his mind and listened, knowing that she'd be trying to communicate with him. It was just up to him to decipher the clues. A comment Ophelia made about the sun visor told him they were going south. Another about the lack of stop signs told him they were heading into the desert. The sound of the engine slowing meant they were slowing to a stop.

"Park there," Gabrielle said.

"By the sandstone caves?" Ophelia said.

But there were hundreds of caves spread like labyrinths across Santa Fe. Which one was she taking her to? Then he heard a rhythmic tapping down the phone line as if Ophelia was drumming her fingers on the steering wheel. Long taps, short taps, deliberate and rhythmic.

It was Morse code. She was giving him the GPS coordinates of where she was.

Hope sprang in his chest.

Hang on, Ophelia, I'm coming for you.

Then he heard a car door open. "What's this?" Gabrielle's voice was suddenly loud down the line as he heard her pick up the phone off the floor. Then he heard the sound of the phone smash against something hard. The call went dead.

He glanced at Meadow.

Worry filled her green eyes. "It's going to be okay. We'll find her."

He hoped so. He plugged the GPS coordinates he thought he'd heard Ophelia tapping out into his phone. A blue dot appeared on the screen, eight miles away to the southwest. He drove toward it, explaining to Meadow as he went what he thought Ophelia had signaled to him.

Desert plains spread out cold and dark in front of his headlights, punctuated by buttes and sandstone outcroppings. A tapestry of bright stars appeared above in the dark sky. He just passed the dot on the screen when he saw Ophelia's car, abandoned and alone at the side of the road.

He pulled over and they leaped out. Meadow grabbed a flashlight from the trunk and started scanning the ground, looking for footprints. Rocky sniffed the air and growled. Pain surged through Kyle's heart. His partner smelled death.

Was he too late? Was Ophelia already gone?

Please Lord, Ophelia can't be dead. She's incredible, smart, caring, beautiful and kind. She's the only woman I've ever been able to imagine spending the rest of my life with and I've just found her. Please, I can't lose her now.

He ran his hand over the dog's side. "Show me," he said softly.

Kyle barked and sniffed the ground, walking this way and that. Then the dog woofed in frustration. Whatever Rocky smelled, it wasn't strong enough to track.

"Do you still have the shirt Ophelia wore?" Meadow said. "I can get Grace to track it."

He pulled it from his jacket pocket and handed it to her. "She only wore it a few hours. Do you think the scent is strong enough?"

In the glow of the flashlight he saw Meadow look down confidently at her K-9 partner. "For Grace? Absolutely."

Kyle stood back and watched as Meadow summoned Grace to her side, instructed her to sniff the shirt Ophelia had worn and track the scent. The vizsla howled and took off running, with Meadow at her side. Kyle and Rocky followed just a few steps behind, as the dog darted this way and that through the towering maze of stone and rock that rose out of the desert.

A cave loomed ahead, like a large mouth in the earth ready to swallow them whole. Rocky barked. Grace howled. The scents both dogs could detect ended in there. The dogs plunged through the opening and into the cave. Meadow and Kyle were on their heels. Her flashlight beams bounced off the walls.

Then he saw them. Ophelia and Gabrielle were down on the ground, battling over a gun. Gabrielle was striking out against Ophelia with all she had, hitting and punching her like a fury. But courage shone brightly in Ophelia's eyes, and he knew she wasn't about to give up easily.

"Down on the ground!" Kyle shouted. "Dorothy Brown,

aka Gabrielle Martinez, you're under arrest for murder and kidnapping."

Gabrielle stumbled back. He watched as her calculating eyes glanced from Kyle to Meadow, and suddenly tears sprang to her eyes.

"You've got to help me!" Gabrielle whimpered and ran toward Meadow. "Ophelia kidnapped me and Kyle is a corrupt cop. They've set me up and they're going to kill me."

"Don't even try." Meadow snorted and raised her gun. "You can't pull that nonsense with me." She ordered Gabrielle to her knees and handcuffed her.

"They don't have any evidence," Gabrielle protested. "It's my word against theirs and Dylan's. No one's going to believe them."

Kyle ran past her and scooped Ophelia up into his arms, even as she collapsed into him as if the last of her fight had finally left her limbs.

"I knew you'd come." She laid her head against his chest. "And that all I had to do was stay alive until you rescued me."

He cupped her face in his hands. "I'm so glad I found you."

"I never had any doubt you would."

He leaned toward her and brushed a kiss across her forehead as she nestled into the crook of his neck. He wanted to tell her that it felt like he'd spent his whole life looking for her without even knowing it, and now that he'd found her, he didn't ever want to let her go.

But before he could even find the words to say, he heard Rocky bark. He turned. The dog was pawing at a duffel bag that lay up against a cave wall.

Ophelia pulled out of his arms. "What did he find?"

"I don't know." Kyle took his phone from his pocket and used it as a flashlight as he walked over to the bag and carefully undid the zipper. Trinkets fell out and clattered on the floor. There was RWN's matching cuff link, the missing piece of Chloe's broken locket, plus an assortment of other rings, necklaces and cuff links, as well as clothing, bundles of cash and multiple driver's licenses and passports.

"It looks like she kept souvenirs of her victims." He sat back on his heels and glanced at Ophelia. "Enough to keep your lab busy for a few days."

He may not have caught the Rocky Mountain Killer, but there was enough evidence in this bag to put a serial killer away for a long time. But as his eyes lingered on Ophelia's face, there was still one question ringing in his heart that he couldn't answer.

Now what?

"See 'oats!" Brody requested loudly and tugged on Ophelia's hand. "Pat now!"

She smiled and looked down at him as they crossed the Cherish Ranch parking lot, feeling a special kind of joy she'd never known before filling her heart. It had been two days since Gabrielle, aka Dorothy, and her brother, Dylan, were arrested and charged with multiple murders, and the manager of Cherish Ranch had agreed to make a meeting room available for investigators to brief ranch staff, Jared and Gabrielle's wedding guests, and select members of the press about the state of the investigation. Ophelia and Kyle had promised to take Brody to the petting zoo after the meeting, along with Alice and her new pharmacist friend. The toddler had no desire to wait.

"We will take Ophelia to see the goats, I promise, buddy,"

Kyle said. He reached down and ruffled the toddler's hair. "Ophelia and I just have to talk to some people first. If you go with Grandma to the kitchen, I hear the chef has made some special cookies."

Brody hesitated. Then nodded.

"Okay," he said.

He dropped Ophelia's hand, patted Rocky on the head, hugged Ophelia's leg tightly and ran toward Alice. He then asked her to pick him up, despite the fact that she was already holding Taffy in her arms.

Ophelia laughed. "I wish I had his energy."

"Don't we all?" Kyle said. Kyle, Ophelia and Rocky watched as the others disappeared though the door to the kitchen. Then he turned to her. "How are you feeling about the briefing?"

"Nervous," she said. "Jared is still refusing to talk to me. He can't believe that the woman he thought he loved was conning him. Thankfully, when police pulled him and Gabrielle aside at the airport, she realized the jig was up, stole a construction vehicle and bailed, leaving Jared with nothing but an empty bank account and a bruised ego. Could've been a lot worse."

"Yeah, but it still has to be a pretty big blow to his ego," Kyle said, "especially for the kind of person who doesn't ever consider he could be wrong."

"Yeah." Ophelia nodded. Her eyes searched the blue sky above. The sound of music floated through the flowering hedges. Someone was having a party in the courtyard. "At least he's agreed to be here today and listen. That's all I can ask."

The briefing was in a small dining room just off the lobby. Sure enough, Jared was there sitting in the back row, beside

Evelyn. She also spotted all the bridesmaids and groomsmen and almost every guest she'd seen at the reception dinner, along with multiple other faces she didn't recognize. Apparently people who'd known Gabrielle had traveled there from Albuquerque, Las Vegas and beyond.

Patricia spoke first, welcoming them all, and then introduced Kyle and Ophelia as the key investigators who'd solved the case.

Kyle quickly went over the basic facts of the case, including Gabrielle's long history of conning people. Dylan had struck a deal with prosecutors and pleaded guilty to helping Gabrielle dispose of Chloe's and Nolan's bodies, tampering with Kyle's vehicle and shooting into the barn. But he said Gabrielle had faked her own kidnapping to con Jared out of more money and that it was Gabrielle who'd fired the fatal shots into Bobby's, Chloe's and Nolan's chests. He claimed he'd only tried to kidnap Ophelia to hold her somewhere until Gabrielle was able to slip out of the hotel unnoticed and kill her herself. Police had since recovered the gun used in all three murders, with her fingerprints on it. As for threatening his sister at gunpoint in the cabin, Dylan claimed he was just looking for the payout she'd promised him.

In a twist that perhaps shouldn't have surprised Ophelia, Gabrielle had confessed as well, no doubt counting on her ability to charm investigators as she'd duped others in the past. In Gabrielle's version of the story, she'd been forced to keep changing her name and moving around the country to escape a long string of bad relationships. She made Bobby out to be a villain who'd discovered her multiple IDs, tried to blackmail her into getting back together with him, and when she'd refused, Bobby had gone to Chloe and convinced her that Gabrielle was a criminal. In her telling, killing Bobby had been an act of self-defense and she'd had no choice but to ask Dylan to kill Chloe. As for Nolan, he'd threatened to tell police that he'd lied when he'd given her an alibi for the time of John Doe's murder.

Kyle was sure neither sibling had told the full truth about their crimes, motives or involvements. But thankfully, they were behind bars now and due to the ongoing, diligent work of law enforcement and the crime lab, they were going to stay there for the rest of their lives.

"I want everyone to know," Kyle said, "that this case would not have been solved without the help of CSI Ophelia Clarke." His voice rose as he looked over the group. Was it her imagination or did his eyes alight specifically on her great-aunt as he spoke? "There's an unfortunate habit some people have of overlooking the people in the background and only focusing on the people running around with the badge and gun. But CSI Clarke is by far the most dedicated and talented crime scene investigator that I have ever worked with. Countless lives have been saved because of her work and the work of people like her." He looked down at her and Ophelia felt a flush rise to her cheeks as he fixed his dark, handsome eyes on her face. "And I mean it when I say, there's nobody else on the planet I'd rather have been partnered with."

Then he turned back to the gathered group.

"I urge you all to focus on the bright side wherever you can find it," Kyle said. "I won't sugarcoat it. This was a grim case and a very sad story. I wish I could say it had a happy ending. But I think we can be thankful for all the hard work the Santa Fe PD, the Mountain Country K-9 Task Force and Crime Scene Unit put into solving it, and all of you who answered questions and helped in the investigation."

He handed the microphone back to Patricia, who started

to brief them on what they could expect to happen next with the case. As Kyle stepped back beside Ophelia, she felt his hand brush her arm. "Let's go for a quick walk, before she opens the floor and people start trying to ask us questions."

"Good idea."

His hand slid down her arm and his fingers linked with hers. Together they slipped out of the back door, with Rocky by their side and back out into the sunshine. There they followed the path through the flowers, toward where the sounds of celebration still rose from the courtyard.

It was a wedding, she realized as they drew closer. Much more modest than what Gabrielle and Jared had planned, but boisterous and full of laughter, as young people and old, from babies to seniors, hugged and celebrated.

They stopped at a rustic bench, not far from the one where she'd sat with Gabrielle just days before. Kyle and Ophelia sat side by side, still holding hands, and with Rocky stretched out of their feet. For a while they just watched the happiness unfolding before them.

"That's what I'd want for my wedding," Kyle said after a long moment. "Nothing expensive or fancy. Just celebrating with people who love me and each other."

"Sounds perfect," Ophelia said. She looked down at their linked hands. His thumb ran gently over her skin. "Do you really believe this story doesn't have a happy ending?"

"This case?" Kyle said. "No. But maybe it can have a happy beginning. Look, I still don't know how you and I are going to make time to get to know each other better, in the middle of everything that's going on in our lives. But how did I put it when we thought I might be running into gunfire? I'm going to stand up, do what I know is right, and trust God to keep us safe and make it all right in the end."

She thought of what Evelyn had said about people lining up at the church to get married on the eve of being shipped off to war because they weren't about to let the hard things in life stop them from the good ones.

"Maybe this isn't the timing I'd have chosen," Kyle said. "But you are the only person I can ever imagine picking to spend my life with. I admired you before we'd even met and now that I know you, you're even more stunning on the inside than you are on the outside." He ran his free hand along her cheek. "I'm falling in love with you and I can't imagine ever letting you go."

A sudden cheer rose from the wedding party and Ophelia looked up to see something flying through the air toward her, over a sea of outstretched hands. Instinctively she pulled away from Kyle and stood. Her arms opened as a huge bouquet of roses and ribbons landed in her hands.

"I think I just caught a wedding bouquet."

Faces from the crowd turned toward her as people laughed, clapped and cheered.

"I think they're waiting for me to do this," Kyle said. He slid off the bench and crouched down on one knee. Rocky cocked his head and watched. Kyle took Ophelia's hand. "I know we've only really known each other a few days, but I have all the evidence I need to know you're the treasure I've secretly been searching for my whole life. I know juggling the busyness of our lives won't be easy. But I have faith that we'll work it out one day at a time together—morning by morning, meal by meal and case by case. And I'd much rather fight to build an amazing life together, than face another day without you by my side. So would you please have dinner with me tonight, go to the park with Brody and me tomorrow, and when we're both ready, will you be please marry me and become by wife?"

Happy tears filled her eyes. "I will."

"I love you, Ophelia."

"I love you, too."

Then his arms went around her waist, she slid her free arm around his neck and their lips met in a kiss that promised a lifetime of joy to come.

* * * * *

If you enjoyed this story, don't miss
Montana Abduction Rescue,
the next book in the Mountain Country K-9 Unit series!

Baby Protection Mission
by Laura Scott, April 2024

Her Duty Bound Defender
by Sharee Stover, May 2024

Chasing Justice
by Valerie Hansen, June 2024

Crime Scene Secrets
by Maggie K. Black, July 2024

Montana Abduction Rescue
by Jodie Bailey, August 2024

Trail of Threats
by Jessica R. Patch, September 2024

Tracing a Killer
by Sharon Dunn, October 2024

Search and Detect
by Terri Reed, November 2024

Christmas K-9 Guardians
by Lenora Worth and Katy Lee, December 2024

Dear Reader,

Well, I had a pretty unusual experience as I was wrapping up this book.

Due to what I'd been told by my usual veterinarian, I believed the kindest thing to do for my beloved dog was to put her down. The surgery she needed was just too unlikely to succeed. Tearfully we drove her to her final sleep. Fittingly, we thought, it was pouring.

When we got there, a different veterinarian seemed astonished that we were there. It turns out our dog's suffering was not due to a serious condition, but a simple one that could be easily treated. She gave us some new prescription samples to try. For now, the dog is responding well to the meds and back to supervising my writing as she has for every book since we rescued her in 2015.

Why am I telling you this? For the simple reason that one of you might one day face a similar situation, remember this story and go to get a second opinion when you need one.

I firmly believe that our stories, good and bad, are one of the greatest gifts that we have to give to the world. Like how Evelyn was able to connect with and help Ophelia on a deeper level when she shared the story of her own wedding, my prayer for is that God will guide you in whom to share your wisdom, experiences, strength and hope with. I also pray that God will bring the right people into your life to share theirs with you.

As always, thank you so much for sharing this journey with me.

Maggie